... ...ge was born in Hull, ...rkshire, ... 1912 and was educated at Bradford Grammar School. He was encouraged at an early age to write by his English teacher and went on to read English at Birmingham University. At the age of twenty-one he sold a radio play to the BBC and continued to write following his graduation whilst working as a stockbroker's clerk.

In 1938, he created the character Paul Temple, a crime novelist and detective. For thirty years the radio serials were hugely successful until the last of the series was completed in 1968. In 1969, Paul Temple was adapted for television and four of the adventures prior to this had been adapted for cinema, albeit with less success than radio and TV. Francis Durbridge also wrote for the stage and continued doing so up until 1991, when *Sweet Revenge* was completed. Additionally, he wrote over twenty other well-received novels, most of which were on the general subject of crime. The last, *Fatal Encounter*, was published after his death in 1998.

Also in this series

FRANCIS DURBRIDGE

Another Woman's Shoes

PLUS

Paul Temple and the Nightingale

WITH AN INTRODUCTION BY
MELVYN BARNES

**COLLINS
CRIME
CLUB**

COLLINS CRIME CLUB

An imprint of HarperCollins*Publishers*
1 London Bridge Street
London SE1 9GF
www.harpercollins.co.uk

This paperback edition 2018

1

First published in Great Britain by Hodder & Stoughton 1965
'Paul Temple and the Nightingale' first published
by Associated Newspapers in *Late Extra: a Miscellany
by 'Evening News' Writers, Artists & Photographers* 1952

Copyright © Francis Durbridge 1965
Introduction © Melvyn Barnes 2018

Francis Durbridge has asserted his right under
the Copyright, Designs and Patents Act, 1988
to be identified as the author of this work

A catalogue record for this book is
available from the British Library

ISBN 978–0–00–827637–9

Typeset in Sabon LT Std by
Palimpsest Book Production Ltd, Falkirk, Stirlingshire

Printed and bound in Great Britain by
CPI Group (UK) Ltd, Croydon CR0 4YY

MIX
Paper from
responsible sources
FSC C007454

This book is produced from independently certified FSC™ paper
to ensure responsible forest management.

For more information visit: www.harpercollins.co.uk/green

Introduction

Harold Weldon has been convicted of the murder of his fiancée Lucy Staines, but crime reporter Mike Baxter is persuaded to investigate further because Lucy's father believes Weldon to be innocent. In particular, Baxter is intrigued by the fact that one of Lucy's shoes is missing, and this becomes crucial when it proves to be the case with further murder victims . . .

In 1965, when *Another Woman's Shoes* was published, devotees of Francis Durbridge will have experienced a feeling of *déjà vu* if they recalled the plot of his radio serial *Paul Temple and the Gilbert Case*. Indeed they would have been justified in doing so, because *Another Woman's Shoes* was the novelisation of that radio serial.

By the 1960s Francis Durbridge (1912–1998) had for many years been arguably the most popular and distinctive writer of mystery thrillers for BBC radio and television, and was soon to make his mark in the theatre. His best-known characters, the novelist-detective Paul Temple and his wife Steve, first appeared in the 1938 BBC radio serial *Send for Paul Temple* and then proceeded to carve their place in broadcasting history in the sequels *Paul Temple and the Front Page*

Men (1938), *News of Paul Temple* (1939), *Paul Temple Intervenes* (1942), *Send for Paul Temple Again!* (1945) and many more. These first five Temple serials soon became books, co-written with John Thewes *(Send for Paul Temple)* and Charles Hatton (the four sequels, although it has been speculated that Thewes was in fact a pseudonym for Hatton), and published by John Long between 1938 and 1948.

Durbridge then went on to produce many more books, including two completely original novels, *Back Room Girl* (1950) and *The Pig-Tail Murder* (1969). With these two exceptions (if you disregard several newspaper serials that he wrote in the 1950s that were never turned into books), his publishing output consisted of two strands: the Paul Temple books and the novelisations of his phenomenally popular television serials. Falling somewhere between the two were the Paul Temple radio scripts that he adapted into non-series novels, now reunited with the canon in these long overdue Collins Crime Club reprints.

Paul Temple and the Gilbert Case was originally broadcast in eight episodes from 29 March to 17 May 1954, and it marked the first of eleven appearances by the actor Peter Coke as Temple. A new production, also with Coke, was recorded and broadcast from 22 November 1959 to 10 January 1960. *Paul Temple and the Gilbert Case* was one of Durbridge's most enthralling radio serials, given its convoluted plot and its denouement exposing a murderer that few listeners would have suspected throughout its eight-week run. Its starting point is an appeal to Temple by Wilfrid Stirling, whose daughter Brenda has been murdered and for which crime her boyfriend Howard Gilbert has been sentenced to death. When Stirling's doubts about the verdict compel Temple to race against time to unravel the mystery before the execution day, the detective is soon faced with more murder victims who (as in Brenda's case) are each lacking a shoe.

As always with Durbridge this radio serial was a huge success, and European countries rushed to cast and broadcast their own versions in straight translations of the original scripts. These included the Dutch *Paul Vlaanderen en het Gilbert mysterie* (3 October to 21 November 1954), the German *Paul Temple und der Fall Gilbert* (4 January to 22 February 1957) and the Danish *Gilbert-mysteriet* (5 July to 23 August 1957).

But why, so soon after the second UK radio production of *Paul Temple and the Gilbert Case*, did Durbridge novelise this serial as *Another Woman's Shoes* and change all the character names, as well as introducing new investigators Mike and Linda Baxter instead of the Temples? Such questions can never be answered with certainty, but it is at least known that with his novels Durbridge tried to widen his appeal to the reading public, in spite of the fact that his radio serials had made him a household name. This diversification was even more evident in other media, with his television serials from 1952 and his stage plays from 1971 completely breaking away from the Temples.

While his early Paul Temple novels in the 1930s and 1940s adhered closely to his radio scripts and characters, this changed in 1951 with two novelisations of radio serials in which all or most of the character names were changed – *Beware of Johnny Washington* and *Design for Murder*, which were originally the radio serials *Send for Paul Temple* (1938) and *Paul Temple and the Gregory Affair* (1946). Indeed, the first 1950s Paul Temple book was another departure, being an original novel rather than a novelisation. *The Tyler Mystery* (1957), published by Hodder & Stoughton.

If the mid-sixties' transformation of *Paul Temple and the Gilbert Case* into the standalone *Another Woman's Shoes* disappointed any Durbridge enthusiasts, it isn't borne out by the sales either at home or abroad. The book was successfully published throughout Europe – in Germany as *Die Schuhe*, in Italy as *La scarpa che mancava sempre*, in the Netherlands as *Wie de schoen past wordt vermoord*, in Spain as *Tres zapatos de mujer* and in Poland as *Buty modelki*. It would prompt Durbridge to apply his art of recycling one more time with his novel *Dead to the World* (1967), which had begun life as the 1951 radio serial *Paul Temple and the Jonathan Mystery* before becoming a non-Temple book with new characters.

The re-publication of *Another Woman's Shoes* and *Dead to the World*, titles that have not been available for half a century, completes the reprinting of all sixteen novels and novelisations featuring or based on the Paul Temple radio series (plus the welcome revival of that rarity, *Back Room Girl*). Also included in this volume is the bonus short story 'Paul Temple and the Nightingale', which first appeared in the Associated Newspapers miscellany volume *Late Extra* in 1952. It provided Durbridge's fans with an extra tale that kept his central character in the public eye and is another demonstration of the author's prolific output in the post-war years.

Melvyn Barnes
September 2017

Chapter One

As far as Press and public were concerned the Weldon case was finished.

Harold Weldon, an impetuous architect in his early thirties, had been tried and found guilty of strangling his fiancée, a fashion model named Lucy Staines. The customary appeal addressed to the Home Secretary had been made, considered, and rejected.

No murder trial can possibly be dull, and the violent death of a beautiful young girl such as Lucy Staines had attracted a fair amount of attention. If the case had failed to reach the bigger newspaper headlines this was in some way due to a particularly nerve-racking international crisis, the kidnapping of a famous TV star's pet poodle, and the audacious daylight robbery of a City bank.

All the same, the Weldon case might have claimed more space on page one had there been a greater element of mystery involved – perhaps a missing corpse, a nation-wide manhunt, or a fascinating trail of clues to whet the appetites of all amateur detectives. But none of these factors had been present. It had all the semblance of an 'open-and-shut case'. One summer's evening before going to the theatre Weldon had been seen and heard quarrelling violently with his fiancée; a few hours later her body had been found near a deserted bomb-site in Soho Square, and a witness had seen Weldon running wildly from the Square shortly after the medically established time of the killing. Harold Weldon had been arrested, the witness had identified him beyond any doubt, the police had found bloodstains on one of his handkerchiefs which he had carelessly left in a suit sent all too hurriedly to the cleaners, and the accused's alibi had failed to stand up to interrogation.

The trial might have gone better for the young architect if he had cut a better figure in Court. Weldon, however, had taken almost palpable pains to rub everyone up the wrong way. His aggressive, sarcastic tongue had not only succeeded in losing him the sympathy of Judge, Jury and public but had eventually upset even his own Defending Counsel. His frequent outbursts of rage, instead of helping to prove his innocence, had only added fuel to the Prosecution's fire – there you have standing before you, it was forcibly hinted, a clear-cut example of a heavily opinionated young man unable to control his violent emotions. The verdict was a foregone conclusion, and there was no popular wave of feeling to support the appeal submitted by Jaime Mainardi, Weldon's Defending Counsel. A date for the hanging had been officially announced; the book containing the story of Harold Weldon's short and stormy life was about to be closed.

This was the precise situation when Mike Baxter, criminologist and ex-Fleet Street crime reporter, entered the case. Interested as he was in all aspects of crime – since they were grist to the mill of the crime articles and books by means of which he earned a very respectable income – he had nevertheless paid the trial only scant attention. His publishers and literary agents were pressing him over the deadline of a book that was overdue, and his wife, Linda, was pressing him to take a holiday which was equally overdue. When the phone rang one morning as he was half-way through typing the final chapter he mentally heaped mild abuse on Linda for being absent and irritably picked up the receiver.

'Conway and Racy's heah,' sang an overbred, fluty, female voice.

'Who?' he muttered. It sounded like a firm of racing bookies. Mike did not go in for gambling, except on certainties.

'Is that the home of Mrs Baxter?' the fluty voice went on.

'My wife's out at the moment,' said Mike politely.

'Oh . . . I see. Well, I wonder if you would be so good as to deliver a message to Modom—'

'I'm very busy. Could you ring again?' Mike cut in, realising that it was his wife's Bond Street dressmakers on the phone.

The smooth female voice faltered. 'I . . . er . . . I don't think you quaite understand, Mr Baxter . . . This is Conway and Racy's of Bond Street—'

'Very well, if it's urgent,' he sighed. 'But make it as brief as you can.'

At that moment he heard the door of his study open and, glancing over his shoulder, saw Linda enter the room.

'. . . Could Modom come for a final fitting tomorrow afternoon?' came the unhappy voice at the end of the wire. 'Perhaps three o'clock would be convenient for Modom?'

'Certainly,' Mike said hastily. 'I'll tell her.'

As he hung up Linda sat down in the leather-upholstered chair opposite his desk and gave him a searching glance.

'What's the matter, Mike?' she said. 'You're looking frustrated.'

'Nothing, darling. Just trying to earn a little honest bread and butter at my typewriter, in between answering calls from your hairdressers, dressmakers and such-like all over Town. Conway and Racy's want you for a fitting at three o'clock tomorrow afternoon.'

'Darling, that's my new suit! The one I'm going away in . . . with you, remember? On holiday, the day after tomorrow. You no doubt recall the arrangements?'

'Yes, dear, I recall.'

Something in his tone make her look up. 'Darling, we *are* going to the South of France as planned, aren't we?'

'Yes, dear.'

'You don't sound very enthusiastic. Just look me square in the eyes and give me your solemn promise—'

'If I am granted just a few hours' undiluted concentration on this laggard opus of mine, we may just about make it.'

Linda stood up, leant forward, and kissed him lightly on the forehead. 'Sorry, darling. I won't disturb you any more. I've a thousand things to do if we're to be ready on time.'

As she turned to go there was a tap on the door, and Mrs Potter, the housekeeper, came in.

'Excuse me, Mr Baxter, but there's a gentleman outside wants to see you.'

Mike groaned. 'Now I know why Dickens never finished *Edwin Drood*. Who is it, Mrs Potter?'

For answer Mrs Potter handed him a small visiting-card.

'Hector Staines, Assistant Sales Director, Keane Brothers,' Mike read out. 'Aren't they the refrigerator people? Tell him we've already got two, Mrs Potter.'

'If you were to ask me, sir, I don't think he wants to sell

you anything. Doesn't talk like a salesman. Seems all het up, says he's got to see you – said something about it being a matter of life and death.'

Mike's eyebrows shot up. 'Did he now? What's he look like?'

'Oh, quite the gent. Tall, grey-haired, frozen-faced type. Walks with a stick. Shouldn't be surprised if he hasn't got a gammy leg.'

Mike exchanged glances with his wife, sighed, and pushed the portable typewriter to one side. 'This obviously is not my morning. You'd better show him in, Mrs Potter.'

'Want me to stay, darling?' Linda asked.

'Maybe you'd better, just in case he starts using his stick when I refuse to buy a fridge.'

Mrs Potter's description of the man who entered the room was, as usual, lacking in respect but remarkably accurate. Obviously public school, Mike found himself thinking as they shook hands, not at all like a refrigerator salesman. And obviously, as Mrs Potter had put it, 'all het up'.

'You'll have to excuse my butting in on you like this,' Staines began, bowing stiffly towards Linda, 'but this is a matter of great urgency.'

'What can I do for you, Mr Staines?' Mike asked politely, glancing at his watch.

'I'll come straight to the point, for I'm sure you're a busy man.'

'He is,' said Linda meaningly.

Mike frowned at her and gestured his visitor to a chair. The elderly man shook his head and began pacing the room nervously. The limp was not very noticeable, but it was there.

'I don't know if you've been following the papers in the past few weeks, Mr Baxter?'

'Not enough to lose any sleep over the international situation. It'll soon blow over.'

'I wasn't referring to politics. I'm talking about the Weldon case. They are going to hang an innocent man.'

'Whom did you say?'

'Harold Weldon.'

Mike glanced at the card in his hand. 'Wait a moment . . . Are you connected with Weldon in some way?'

'Yes. Lucy Staines was my only daughter,' said the visitor quietly.

There was silence in the room for several seconds. Then Mike said: 'From what I remember of the case you were one of the principal witnesses *against* Weldon. Your evidence helped convict him, didn't it?'

'I am aware of the paradox,' the elderly man answered shortly. 'That's what makes it all so damnedly . . . difficult. I have no very great sympathy for the young man, but I don't think he killed my daughter. Not any more.'

'Just one moment, Mr Staines, before we go any farther. I think I should tell you, whatever you may have heard to the contrary, that I'm not connected with Scotland Yard in any official capacity. If you have any fresh evidence which makes you think Weldon is innocent, then it's your duty to go to the police without a moment's delay.'

'That's just it,' Staines answered, his stiff features crumpling into an expression of unhappy despair. 'I don't have any fresh evidence, at least not to speak of.'

'Then what exactly brings you here?'

'Simply that I don't believe any more that he was the murderer.'

'He was given a fair trial before Judge and Jury, wasn't he? The verdict appears to be clear enough.'

6

'Juries can make a mistake. It has been known to happen. Mostly they find out when it's already too late.'

Mike nodded thoughtfully. 'True enough. But I fear the Home Secretary would hardly find this intuition of yours sufficient grounds for reopening the case. Will you be a bit more explicit? You must have something to go on or you wouldn't have bothered to come and see me.'

Staines broke off his pacing up and down and sank into a chair, his head sunk low on his chest, the stick at his side. He had obviously been bred in the strict school where to show one's emotions is a crime of the worst possible taste. His rather high voice was strained and impersonal and he did not look up as he spoke.

'I suppose it's partly my conscience that is driving me. When you lose your only daughter, Mr Baxter, the world collapses like a shattered building around you. The shock is quite indescribable.'

'I'm sure it is,' said Linda sympathetically.

'When the shock recedes, there is a terrible reaction, an urge to lash out, a burning desire for revenge. A voice cries out inside you – "Someone must be made to pay for this!"'

There was another tense silence, which Mike broke, speaking quietly but clearly. 'Are you trying to tell me you gave false evidence against your proposed son-in-law, Mr Staines?'

'Good God, no! I told the truth, as I had sworn to do, in answer to all the questions put to me.'

'The truth as you saw it at that time?'

'Since then, since the verdict, I've lain awake at nights, worrying about that unfortunate young man sitting in the death cell, waiting for the hangman's steps. And my conscience torments me – was it *my* evidence that put him there? My daughter is gone, nothing can bring her back to me . . . but have I the right to add another death to the misery that has already occurred?'

'Surely,' said Mike, choosing his words carefully, 'you have nothing to reproach yourself with? You only did your duty, unpleasant though it must have been.'

'I've tried telling myself that. It doesn't help. I keep going over it all in my mind.'

Linda and Mike exchanged glances as the elderly man buried his face in his hands.

Linda said, 'Mr Staines, my husband and I have been rather busy of late, so we didn't follow the trial as closely as some people. Would you tell us exactly what happened on the night of the murder?'

Staines lifted his head and the pain was clearly visible in his pale grey eyes. 'Harold and Lucy had been engaged for about six months and were going to get married next spring. They saw quite a lot of each other, as much as their respective jobs would permit. Harold is a junior partner in a firm of architects. I don't much care for his work, it's too modernistic; he seems to regard himself as a sort of angry young man of design, but that's neither here nor there. Lucy, as perhaps you know, earned her living as a fashion model. She loved her work, every bit as much as he did his. On the night she was killed they had a dinner appointment, with a theatre to follow. Harold called at the house for her around six o'clock. I should perhaps explain that Lucy and I had lived alone since my wife died during the Blitz. I offered them both a drink, then I had to go upstairs on some errand or other, and I heard them talking. Their voices grew rather heated and it was soon clear they were having a fair-sized row. It was not the first quarrel they had had.'

'Could you hear what they were talking about?'

'Shouting, not talking.'

'And what was the topic of the quarrel?'

'The same thing they always fought about: Harold wanted Lucy to give up her job once they were married. She refused. She loved the work, and quite frankly liked the money; it's a firm that pays very well. Lucy always insisted that she was going to stay on there after they got married. It was a big thorn between them and neither was willing to give in. Lucy always was a high-spirited, independent sort of girl and Harold is too self-opinionated ever to be able to see anyone else's point of view. It was an ugly row and frankly I was glad when they left the house to go to the theatre, or rather to have dinner first.'

'What time was that?'

'About a quarter to seven. As it happened, some people we know saw them at the restaurant, and they also bumped into some chance acquaintances at the theatre. Apparently they hadn't patched things up. It must have been an unpleasant sort of evening. I expect you know the rest of the story: early next morning the police found Lucy strangled on a demolition-site in Soho. Harold tried to lie about his alibi but the police tripped him up. He had to retract his first statement. He was quite unable to give a satisfactory account of his actions between leaving the theatre and the time of the murder.'

'I seem to remember the tangle he got into over his alibi,' Mike put in.

'Mr Staines, may I ask you something?' Linda said. 'Did your daughter have any close friends?'

'If you mean was she consorting with other young men, the answer is no,' came the blunt reply. 'Weldon's smarmy

9

Counsel tried to insinuate something like that but he had no proof.'

'I was thinking more of girlfriends, actually.'

'Oh, I see. Yes, she saw quite a lot of another young girl who also works as a model at the same place in Bond Street.'

'Do you know the girl's name?' Mike asked.

Staines appeared to consider for a moment, at the same time taking out his white pocket handkerchief and mopping his brow. 'I believe her name is Peggy Bedford. Something like that.'

Linda cut in quickly. 'You mentioned Bond Street just now. Did the girls work for one of the bigger establishments?'

'Conway and Racy's.'

Mike's eyebrows shot up and Linda gave a slightly shaky laugh.

'How odd,' she muttered, but Staines, standing up as if to leave, dropped his stick and missed her reaction as he bent to pick it up.

'I know you must feel I'm wasting your time, Mr Baxter,' he said, 'but I just had to unburden myself to someone. I cannot sleep at nights.'

'You've really given me very little to go upon, you know. Even if I had the time, which I haven't, I fail to see what there is I can do.'

'You could try and find L. Fairfax for a start,' the elderly man replied abruptly.

'L. Fairfax? Who is that?'

'The person with whom Lucy had an appointment on May 12th. It was found in her diary.'

'The police know of this?'

'It came out at the trial. They made a half-hearted attempt to find him, or her, but I got the feeling no one was particularly interested. Things might have been different if May 12th had been the date of her death, but as it was a few days afterwards no one seemed to find the entry significant.'

'Was the entry in her own handwriting?'

'Yes. "L. Fairfax. 8.30," it said.'

'Beyond all doubt?'

'Definitely.'

'I see. Well, if you really think you have told us all you can, Mr Staines . . .' said Mike, rising and glancing at his wristwatch.

Staines gave him a sharp look and seemed on the point of challenging the remark, then thought better of it, nodded politely to Linda, shook hands, and left.

'What did you make of him, darling?' Linda asked as they sat some time later over lunch.

'What did you?' he countered with a grin.

'Come off it, I asked first. Though if you want my opinion I think Hector Staines is a bit unbalanced.'

'Interesting. In what way does he strike you as odd?'

'Well, for one thing, did you notice how awkwardly he behaved when I asked him about his daughter's friends? Almost as if I had asked him how big his bank overdraft is or something.'

Mike nodded reflectively.

'Good for you. If I were interested in this case' – he held up a hand as if to ward off Linda's grimace of alarm – 'I only said *if*. But if I were interested and didn't know quite where to start, I think I would fancy a little talk with Miss Peggy Bedford, employee of that well-known and somewhat pricey firm in Bond Street.'

Linda laughed. 'You know perfectly well I've got an

appointment there at three o'clock tomorrow. Now, of course, you'll play the gallant husband and insist on driving me there and picking me up.'

'Darling, you malign me. I only said *if* I were interested in the Weldon case.'

He pretended to busy himself with his dessert, but after a moment continued thoughtfully, 'There's another person I should like to confront with a few pointed questions: Mr Staines himself. The grounds he gave for wanting to see me were just too flimsy for words. And another thing: do you remember exactly what he said when he was talking about having given evidence against Weldon?'

'Something about . . . "I told the truth as I had sworn to do", wasn't it?'

'That wasn't all; he added a rider. "In answer to all the questions they put to me", I think he said.'

Mike had spoken the last phrase with deliberate emphasis and watched his wife to see their effect.

'Wait a moment! You mean he answered to nothing except what he was asked?'

'Exactly! We may be jumping to conclusions but Hector Staines gives me the impression of a man not entirely at ease with himself, not at ease with his inner voice, not at ease with what he has told and *what he has not told*. I think it might be the last bit that is grating on his nerves. Why else should he come to see me, instead of going to Weldon's lawyer or the police, at the eleventh hour?'

'That's easy: because he realises he has nothing concrete to go on. A blind man can see that it'll not do Harold Weldon a bit of good shouting about his supposed innocence from the rooftops; one has to have some hard facts. Staines has none to offer, therefore there's no point in bothering the police.'

12

'I'm with you part of the way. But supposing, just for the sake of argument, that Staines has not called in the Law because he himself is just a wee bit scared of them? I know this is pure surmise but just suppose he's scared to have too many stones uplifted, too many private alleys peered into.'

Linda burst out laughing. 'Darling, you're getting your metaphors all mixed up, and what's more, I don't like that gleam in your eye at all. Finish your lunch and think about that deadline before we can get away on holiday. The Weldon case is not for you.'

Mike grinned and turned to his plate once more.

Over coffee, which Mrs Potter brought in later, he said casually: 'Doing anything special this afternoon?'

Linda snorted. 'I know exactly what *that* introductory gambit means. And you know perfectly well I have a thousand and one different things to do. Packing, for instance.'

'When I think of the size of that bikini you're planning to wear in Cannes I fail to see how it's going to take you very long to pack.'

Linda frowned. 'All right, darling, what's on your mind?'

'Just an idea that you might give your old friend Sammy Spears on the *Tribune* a tinkle and get him to talk about the Weldon case.'

'Sammy Spears?'

'Yes, dear. He's still their ace crime reporter, isn't he? He's bound to have covered the trial. Don't blush, darling, he *was* one of your more ardent admirers in the old days.'

'Sammy Spears was just—'

'Splendid! So do your stuff and see what you can get from him, will you? Rather than spend my valuable time trudging round Fleet Street reference libraries I'd much prefer to let your old boyfriends do my homework for me.'

'What exactly do you hope to get out of Sammy?'

'I'm not quite sure. Put it this way: Sammy's a good journalist and a very bright boy and I'd be interested in hearing anything he has to tell me about the case. Literally anything. The facts, the rumours, his general impression, any hunches or private conclusions he came to and couldn't write about, what he thought of the principal figures in the case, and so on.'

'And if Sammy says Harold Weldon got what was coming to him?'

'Then I'll take Sammy's word for it and drop the matter.'

It was later that evening as Mike was mixing dry martinis in a tall pitcher – don't bruise the gin with a noisy shaker, introduce it to the vermouth with loving care in a slender jar, Mike always maintained – that Linda burst somewhat breathlessly into their Sloane Street flat and apologised for being late.

'Drink, darling?' he asked.

'Thanks, no. I've had more than my ration with Sammy. You know how it is with my late colleagues – nothing under half an hour at El Vino's will get them to so much as open their mouths.'

'And how long were you at El Vino's?'

Linda grinned guiltily. 'One hour and three-quarters. I thought I might as well make the most of it, since you told me I could go out with an old admirer.'

'I sense a strain of female logic that is likely to baffle me coming up. Did Sammy get around to talking about the Weldon case?'

'He did.' Linda sighed heavily and lit cigarettes for them both.

'Why the dramatic sigh?' Mike asked.

'Because I'm having a battle with my conscience. What Sammy told me was not at all what I wanted to hear, but I regret to say it'll be food and drink to you.'

'I'm all ears.'

'Well, this is strictly off the record, and of course Sammy couldn't print a word of it unless he wanted to face about twenty-five libel suits, but in his opinion it was a mis-trial.'

Mike whistled softly. 'That is a big statement, coming from Sammy. Go on, dear, you begin to intrigue me.'

'That's what I was afraid of,' Linda said dryly. 'However, I imagine you'll drag it out of me one way or another. Why was it a mis-trial? Well, partly on account of the Judge, who seems to have been half senile and should have been put out to grass years ago. The Jury also struck Sammy as being more than usually bovine. But the prize ass of them all, apparently, was Jaime Mainardi, QC, Harold Weldon's defending lawyer. In Sammy's opinion the man made a terrible hash of the case. It's not the sort of thing you can put in a newspaper article, but it really does seem as though there was an underlying antagonism between Mainardi and Weldon throughout the whole of the trial.'

'Between Defence Counsel and client? That *is* unusual.'

'Exactly. One expects the Prosecution to clash swords with the accused, but not the two who are supposedly sitting on the same side of the Court. General opinion appears to label this man Weldon as an awkward sort of cuss, but by all accounts he was extraordinarily badly handled. Mainardi sounds a terrible ham, playing to the gallery all the time regardless of the inept job he was making of defending his client.'

15

'It would be rather interesting, one can't help thinking, to have a short talk with Mr Jaime Mainardi, QC,' said Mike musingly.

'That's what Sammy suggested. Mainardi has chambers just off Chancery Lane,' said Linda in a flat, resigned voice, groping in her handbag for a piece of paper. 'Sammy looked up the address for me.'

Mike coughed with mild embarrassment but did not take the proffered slip of paper. 'Thanks, but I've already got the address. Don't glare at me, darling, I finished my writing stint and I had to fill my time doing something whilst waiting for you.'

'Mike Baxter, you promised me you wouldn't get involved in this case,' she reminded him.

'Nor will I, darling, so you go right ahead packing that tiny bikini for Cannes, and we'll set off just as soon as I've got one or two little things tied up.'

Mike walked over to the phone and dialled a number.

Linda said, 'You don't expect to find barristers in their chambers at this time of the evening, do you?'

'Certainly not. I'll catch him tomorrow morning.'

'Then who are you ringing, darling?'

'Oh, just a call to Superintendent Goldway,' said Mike with a grin. He turned to the telephone again at the sound of a familiar voice. 'Hello, is that you, John? Mike Baxter here. Sorry to bother you, but I wonder if you could help me out on a small matter? . . . Could you get one of your departments to check up on the existence or non-existence of a pub, hotel, club, or similar type of meeting place named the Lord Fairfax? . . . Yes, Fairfax . . . Say within a rough fifty-mile radius of London? . . . No, I can't tell you now, but I might be very grateful for five minutes of your time tomorrow morning . . . Splendid! I'll give you a ring, if I may? . . . Thank you so much. Good night.'

Linda said, still in the same flat voice tinged with irony, 'You *have* been doing some thinking, haven't you, darling? And there was I, happy in the thought of you all afternoon, nose hard at the old grindstone, winding up the last chapter.'

'The book's nearly finished. As for this Fairfax idea, it's just a mild speculation. Probably nothing in it at all. But I did wonder whether, instead of hunting amongst a nation of some fifty million souls for a mysterious gent by the name of L. Fairfax, whether it might not be worth looking for a *place* of that name, perhaps a pub or hotel, where Lucy Staines had an appointment on May 12th at eight-thirty.'

'I have to admit it sounds logical enough.'

'And if we draw a blank, well then, there's nothing more to it, is there?'

'I seem to have heard that line before, Mr Baxter. When you start sniffing like an old war-horse at the sound of battle I know exactly what I'm in for. Involvement lies just around the corner.'

'Darling, take your skates off, you're going much too fast! I'm not involved in the Weldon case at all. Everybody agrees it's finished.'

Linda sniffed with open disbelief. 'I know how you enjoy being odd man out,' she said.

Chapter Two

Mike turned right from Chancery Lane into the Strand and searched irritably for a taxi amongst the whirling traffic. It was a lovely late summer's morning but in the mood he was in he was totally incapable of taking pleasure in the polished sunlight gleaming on the red double-decker buses and glancing off traffic and shop windows along the busy street.

His interview with Jaime Mainardi, QC, had been brief and infuriating. With difficulty he had kept control of his temper. Sammy Spears had been right, the man was a ham and should never have been engaged to defend a difficult client like Harold Weldon. Whether Weldon was guilty of murder or not Mike Baxter had not the faintest idea; but after his short, exasperating interview with Weldon's legal brains Mike was ready to side with at least one of Sammy Spears's theories, that the accused had been extraordinarily badly handled.

What had appalled Mike more than anything else was Mainardi's bland acceptance of his client's fate. It must no doubt be galling for a lawyer to lose a case, but this was no ordinary divorce wrangle or libel suit: a man's life had hung in the balance, the death penalty had been pronounced. He had expected to find some traces of regret, if not deep remorse, in Mainardi's chambers but all he had sensed was calm indifference.

He hailed a taxi, told the driver to take him to Scotland Yard, and climbed in.

Mainardi's astonishingly urbane summing up as he brought the brief interview to an end still resounded in his ears. 'Really, Mr Baxter, you must excuse me if I cannot give you very much of my time, but I am a business man like any other and my bread and butter is earned by accepting briefs from new clients, not in trying to console clients whose cases I have unfortunately lost.' And then, to crown it all, the man had had the effrontery to ask, in a far from delicate manner, just how soon payment of his legal fees might be expected.

'No doubt you'll get paid before they put the rope round Weldon's neck,' Mike had snapped.

The barrister had popped his cheeks dramatically and laid an eloquent hand to his forehead, as if he were affronted by Mike's abruptness. 'Forgive me for saying so, Mr Baxter, but for my part I cannot quite understand what your interest in this case is.'

'For my part,' Mike had replied, 'I'm just beginning to understand. Good day.'

As the taxi wound its way down Whitehall, Mike forced himself to cool down. The fact that Weldon's defence had been placed in the hands of a slipshod ham by no means proved the architect's innocence. The same verdict might have been returned had he been superbly defended. Yet Mike found himself probing deeper and deeper into the affair, unable to resist (as Linda had put it) the whiff of cannon-fire and the sound of distant battle. Most of all he felt an imperative urge to meet Harold Weldon in person. As he paid off

19

his taxi and entered the Yard he was wondering if Goldway could arrange a visit to Pentonville.

The Sergeant on duty knew Mike well and after the usual formalities he was shown upstairs to Goldway's room overlooking the river.

The tall, white-haired, distinguished-looking Superintendent was busy on the telephone as Mike entered, but shot him a welcoming smile and waved him to a vacant chair. When the phone call ended Goldway stood up and shook hands, offering Mike a cigarette and inquiring after Linda's health. Knowing the pressure under which Goldway worked Mike came straight to the point and told him of Hector Staines's visit which had prompted his first stirrings of interest in the Weldon case.

'I know it doesn't sound very much to go on, John, but the truth is I've nibbled at the bait and now I can't quite let go.'

'Always was a chronic weakness of yours, Mike,' said Goldway with a benevolent smile. 'However, we've been glad enough of your assistance in times gone by, so I think the least I can do now is to offer some co-operation when you ask for it. I must point out, purely as a formality, that the Weldon case is officially closed, of course.'

'Of course. But to a dyed-in-the-wool criminologist like myself no case is ever fully closed. We're still arguing about some of the verdicts of the eighteenth century; and in this case the condemned man still has a week or two to live.'

'Quite so. Let's say your interest is purely academic. Now about this Lord Fairfax notion of yours; I've put some good men on running it to earth if it does exist, and I should think they'll come up with a definite answer before the day is out.'

Mike looked crestfallen. 'No word yet? I was hoping for

a lead there. Supposing my theory is accurate and the Fairfax is a pub or something, instead of a person, it would be rather intriguing to know just whom Lucy Staines was planning to meet there, wouldn't it?'

'Possibly. But I wouldn't bank on it if I were you. As far as visiting Weldon in Pentonville goes, I can arrange that for you if you insist, though I don't think you'll find him much of a charmer. The man has a positively fiendish talent for getting one's back up. There's another man you might like to meet, though, who could be useful.'

'Who's that?'

'Detective-Inspector Charles Rodgers. He was in charge of the case.' Goldway picked up the internal telephone and spoke quietly into it, adding aside to Mike, 'Don't expect him to be delighted to make your acquaintance either; he's a busy fellow and right up to his neck in a vicious stabbing case at the Elephant and Castle at the moment. I'll see if he can spare us a minute.'

Rodgers proved available and arrived within a few minutes of Goldway's summons. Mike's impression as he shook hands with the Inspector was of a tough, hard-driving, and extremely efficient man in his middle forties, a careless dresser, heavy smoker (from the nicotine stains on his fingers), a man of few words, in love with his job to the exclusion of most other interests.

Goldway completed the introductions with, 'As I said, Mike, Rodgers was in charge of the case.'

'Right from the beginning, Inspector?' Mike asked.

'Yes.'

'I see. The snag is, I wasn't at the trial,' Mike went on, 'so I don't know all the details. I know Weldon and his fiancée had a bad row – Staines told me all about that – and

21

then they went to dinner and to the theatre. What exactly happened after that?'

Rodgers's mouth tightened in a slight grimace of annoyance and he glanced rather obviously at his watch.

Goldway put in smoothly, 'I don't think this will take more than five minutes of your time, Inspector. Mike is an old friend of mine, and I've told him how pushed you are lately.'

Rodgers grunted and rubbed the palm of his hand hard on his short-clipped hair. 'Very well,' he said. 'Weldon and Lucy Staines left the theatre before the show finished, at about ten o'clock. According to Weldon's first statement their quarrel came to a climax outside the theatre and Lucy turned her back on him and walked away. Weldon got into his car and drove home. He said – mark you, this was his *first* statement – that he arrived home at about half-past ten.'

'Weldon had a flat in New Cavendish Street which he shared with a friend named Victor Sanders,' Goldway put in.

'Sanders failed to confirm Weldon's story,' the Inspector continued. 'He said that Weldon didn't get home till about half-past twelve. We tackled Weldon on this point and he changed his statement. He said he left Lucy outside the theatre at ten o'clock, drove round the West End a bit, parked his car in St James's Square, and then went for a walk. He says he got back to the Square at about a quarter-past twelve. That's practically a two-hour walk, you'll note. Then he got in his car and drove home. No one saw him, and no one saw the car.'

'In other words he couldn't account very convincingly for his movements between ten o'clock and twelve-thirty,' Mike said.

'Quite so,' Goldway answered. 'Medical opinion has established beyond all doubt that it was during this period that the murder took place. Go on, Inspector.'

'Two days after the murder Weldon sent a suit to be sponged and pressed. I went to see the cleaners and found a handkerchief in one of the pockets. It had blood on it. The blood was tested and found to belong to the same group as the murdered girl's. Weldon admitted it was his handkerchief, but he couldn't account for the blood.'

'Excuse me . . . but I thought Lucy Staines was strangled?'

'She was. But she must have put up some kind of a struggle. There was a bad scratch down the side of her face. That accounted for the blood.'

'Who discovered the body, Inspector?'

'A woman called Nadia Tarrant. She has a flat in Soho Square. She was taking a short cut across the bomb-site just after midnight when a man came out of the shadows, pushed past her, and ran down Greek Street. She was able to give us a description of the man and we put Harold Weldon amongst others in an identity parade. She picked him out without a moment's hesitation. We also found Weldon's fingerprints on Miss Staines's handbag. There were five pounds in the purse and a gold powder compact. Also she was wearing a nice little diamond clip.'

'Was anything missing?' Mike asked.

'No. That ruled out assault with intent to rob.'

Goldway interrupted as Rodgers lit himself a cigarette. 'There was actually one thing missing, oddly enough. But it doesn't appear to be relevant.'

'Why, John? What was it?'

'Her shoe.'

Rodgers blew out a cloud of smoke and nodded. 'Yes, I

forgot that. She was only wearing one shoe, on her right foot. The other must have fallen off during the struggle. Strangely enough we never found it.'

Mike frowned thoughtfully. 'What a curious thing for a murderer to take. What use is one shoe? Could be damning evidence too.' He caught Inspector Rodgers looking at his watch and said hastily, 'Inspector, you've been very generous with your time. Many thanks for putting me in the picture.'

Rodgers nodded surlily and left with a curt, 'Good day.'

On leaving the Yard Mike took a taxi to his garage where his car, a new E-type Jaguar, was being given a grease-job, then drove in deep thought back to Sloane Street where a cold lunch prepared by Linda and served by Mrs Potter awaited him.

That afternoon, mindful of his deadline, he thrust all thought of the Weldon case out of his head and put in a good two hours' work on his book. The only interruption was a telephone message from Linda telling him not to expect her back at the flat and asking him to pick her up at Conway and Racy's some time after three o'clock.

Finding a place to park near Bond Street was hopeless but eventually Mike saw a gap in Hanover Square and dived at it like a Rugby wing forward, beating two rivals by sheer effrontery and superior acceleration. By the time he had walked to Conway and Racy's Linda had finished her final fitting for the two-piece grey suit she referred to as her 'Cannes stunner'. It would be delivered on the following day and Mike grimly reminded himself that the bill was likely to be a stunner too.

'How did you fare at the Yard?' Linda asked him as she came out of the changing booth.

'Only so-so.'

'You look depressed. Haven't they found a Lord Fairfax hotel?'

He shook his head. 'Not only that; my brief chat with Mr Jaime Mainardi was enough to put a blight on the day. I'll tell you all about it once I've steered you successfully past the hat department and out of this criminally expensive emporium.'

Linda giggled and took his arm. 'Too late, darling, I've already visited the hat department.'

Mike sighed heavily. 'What did you buy? – Two feathers, and a wisp of veil direct from Paris?'

'Nothing as bad as that, honestly.' She turned for support to a well-groomed blonde assistant in her late thirties who was hovering near by and making vaguely helpful gestures; she was obviously the Department Supervisor who had arranged Linda's fitting. She favoured Mike with an exceedingly arch smile that involved a lot of teeth and brilliant lipstick. Linda introduced her as Miss Long.

'I think you'll like the hat, Mr Baxter. It really looks most *distinguée* on your wife.'

'You're the expert,' said Mike. 'Oh, by the way, Miss Long, do you have a young lady working here, as a model, I think, by the name of Peggy Bedford?'

Miss Long hesitated for a second, then said, 'Yes, we do. She's in the lingerie department.'

'I wonder if I might have a word with her?'

'By all means, Mr Baxter. The only trouble is, she's not here today.'

'Is she ill?'

'No; at least I don't think so.'

'You don't happen to know where I might be able to contact her?'

A fleeting shadow of doubt crossed the blonde assistant's face and Linda stepped gallantly to the rescue. 'Don't worry, Miss Long, if she's too attractive I'll keep my husband on a very short leash.'

Miss Long giggled nervously. 'Well, it isn't usual, of course, but in the circumstances there's really no reason why I shouldn't give you her address. She has a flat in Plymouth Mansions, just off Baker Street. She's probably there; our models sometimes work very irregular hours.'

'Thank you, you've been most kind. I believe Peggy Bedford was a close friend of Lucy Staines, wasn't she?'

Miss Long's expression changed. 'Er . . . yes, that is so. What a dreadful business that was. It cast the most fearful gloom over – Oh, excuse me, Mr Baxter, there's the house phone, I must answer it. Goodbye, Mrs Baxter, I do hope you have a lovely holiday.'

Outside in Bond Street Mike took his wife's arm and led her to where the car was parked in Hanover Square.

'Are we going straight home, darling?' Linda asked.

'More or less. With a little detour via Baker Street, if you don't mind.'

'Peggy Bedford? What do you hope to get out of her?'

'Maybe she can shed some light on who L. Fairfax was, assuming my original hunch was wrong. At least she should be able to give me some idea of Lucy Staines's habits, her interests, what sort of circles she moved in.'

They drove to Baker Street and after several fruitless inquiries succeeded in finding Plymouth Mansions. It was an imposing building set some distance off the main street. Linda's eyes widened as she stepped out of the car and gazed at the impressive entrance.

'Rather an expensive address for a fashion model, isn't it?' Mike said, running his finger down the list of tenants' names in the entrance hall.

'I suppose we shouldn't be too surprised. Staines said the girls earn good money.'

He quickly found the name he wanted. 'Here we are! – Peggy Bedford. Flat 37. We'll take the lift, unless you want to climb three flights.'

A surly, uniformed porter with a permanent scowl took them up and gruffly jerked his head towards the corridor leading to Flat 37.

Mike pressed the bell and they waited in silence. No answering steps came. They rang again, and after a few moments Linda bent impatiently to try to peer through the keyhole.

'That's odd,' she muttered, 'it's plugged with paper or something.' She dropped on one knee and sniffed at the base of the door. Then she exclaimed in alarm, 'Mike, I think I smell gas!'

Mike dropped quickly to the floor and confirmed her suspicion. 'Linda, get that porter as quickly as you can! Tell him to bring a pass-key!'

Throwing his weight against the door he tried to burst in, but it was well constructed and resisted his efforts. A few seconds later came the sound of the lift doors opening and Linda ran down the corridor towards him waving the key.

'He refused to give it to me so I just grabbed it and ran. I told him to phone for an ambulance.'

'Fine. Hold your breath – here goes!'

Holding a handkerchief in front of his mouth and nose Mike swung open the door and groped his way towards a dimly visible window. He heaved it open and found he was in the kitchen. All the taps of the gas oven were on and he quickly shut them off.

As he turned his heel stepped on something soft . . . It was the hand of a woman whose body lay partly concealed under the kitchen table. Coughing back the fumes he made for the window, then returned once more and managed to lift the body. Choking for breath he dragged her through the hall and outside into the corridor. With Linda's help he began trying to revive the girl.

'Keep her head up high, darling.'

'Where the hell is that ambulance?'

'It'll be here in a minute. Do you think she's dead?'

'Pretty close, I should say. If that porter doesn't get a move on she won't have much chance.'

They heard shouts and running footsteps which grew nearer. A small crowd of excited onlookers, led by the porter, rushed up.

'Did you phone for an ambulance? Is there a doctor handy?' Mike shouted, waving them away from the girl.

The porter gulped nervously and managed to croak some sort of affirmative.

'Do you know this girl?' Linda asked him.

The porter nodded and his Adam's apple jerked convulsively. 'It's the Bedford tart, Flat 37. Always did say she'd come to no good, I did.'

'Never mind that now!' Mike cried. 'Help me carry her out into the fresh air. Come on, what are you dithering about?'

Whilst the porter was still muttering to himself, other, more capable, hands from amongst the crowd helped Mike carry the girl to the lift and swiftly down and out into the fresh air.

Above the howl of a siren and the clangour of an approaching ambulance bell Mike said angrily to Linda, 'What the blazes was that fool muttering about? Is something missing?'

'You could say that,' replied Linda, looking down at the inert figure.

He followed her glance and saw that the girl was wearing only one shoe.

Chapter Three

Mike Baxter and Linda were lost in deep thought as they drove back to their flat. They were none too pleased to find that they had a visitor waiting for them.

Mrs Potter was very apologetic. 'Tried to send him on his way, I did, but he wouldn't budge. I've put him in the study.'

'All right, Mrs Potter. What did you say his name is?'

'Mr Victor Sanders, he says. Never set eyes on him before and I don't care how long it is before—'

'Do you know him, Mike?' Linda interrupted.

'I heard the name for the first time this morning. It could be the fellow Harold Weldon shared a flat with in New Cavendish Street. All right, Mrs Potter, ask him to come in.'

The man Mrs Potter showed into the room was tall, extremely well dressed, and completely self-assured. His voice when he spoke seemed unnaturally loud for the size of the room they were in.

'My name is Victor Sanders,' he boomed, fixing Mike Baxter with a piercing glare. 'I'm sure your time is as valuable as mine, so I'll come straight to the point.'

'One moment,' Mike put in quietly. 'Before you go on, may I introduce my wife?'

Sanders turned slightly towards Linda, nodded curtly, and went on talking. All too plainly in his opinion women should be seen and not heard. His manner suggested a colonel on parade and his complexion was an appropriate red, though whether it resulted from too hearty bellowing or too heavy drinking was hard to tell.

'Baxter, I understand you saw Inspector Rodgers about the Weldon case this morning?'

'You are remarkably well informed, *Mister* Sanders,' Mike replied, placing careful emphasis on the polite form of address which their visitor apparently scorned.

'I make a point of being well informed about anything that could possibly have a bearing on the Weldon case.'

'Really? You interest me.'

Sanders nodded arrogantly. 'As you are doubtless aware, Weldon shared my flat until this unfortunate business occurred. I knew him pretty well. And I have a theory about the whole case which is going to make you sit up and take notice.'

'I rather think Inspector Rodgers is the man you ought to take your theories to, Mr Sanders.'

Sanders made a curtly dismissive gesture with one hand. 'I've already discussed it with him at great length. The man's obtuse, can't see beyond his own nose.'

Mike replied, 'In all fairness I must tell you that was not at all my impression of the Inspector. He struck me as a very conscientious—'

Sanders cut in impatiently, 'Hector Staines came to see you yesterday, didn't he, Baxter?'

'Were you behind the curtain?' Mike retorted, faintly nettled despite his inner resolve to keep a tight curb on his tongue.

'Staines told you about the entry in his daughter's diary, I imagine?'

'What do you know about her diary?' put in Linda.

Sanders favoured her with a cold glare that scarcely checked his booming flow. 'Staines's daughter had an appointment with a man called Fairfax at eight-thirty on May 12th.'

'We don't know that for certain,' Mike began.

'Nonsense! It's there in black and white in the diary.'

'The words are there, certainly.'

'Let's not split hairs, Baxter. I told you my time is valuable.'

Linda could not control an exclamation, but Sanders swept on, ignoring her completely. 'It is my theory that Lucy Staines was having an affair with this man Fairfax, and that he followed her to the theatre that night.'

'That's pure supposition, unless you have some proof,' Mike said.

Sanders smiled complacently and pulling out his wallet he extracted a letter. 'Here, read this!' he snapped. 'It came by the afternoon post. As you see, it's postmarked Como, Italy, four days ago.'

Mike took the letter and glanced at the address. 'It appears to be addressed to Harold Weldon, not to you, Mr Sanders.'

'Quite. But our address is the same and Harold is in prison, so naturally I opened it.'

'Naturally,' Linda remarked.

Mike pulled out the sheet of airmail paper and studied the typewritten contents:

Dear Harold,
    So now it is all over, and they have found you guilty.
I wonder whether you really did murder Lucy Staines?

I met you once, a long time ago – I expect you've forgotten. When I heard about the murder and read the reports and saw Lucy's photograph in the newspapers, I said to myself, 'There, but for the Grace of God . . .' Dear Lucy, such a lovely creature – but not an easy person to get on with, was she? I wonder if you just happened to be the unlucky one they've picked on. I wonder! Was her shoe missing, Harold? Ask the police, it might be worth your while. Good luck to you, Harold . . . heaven knows, you need it.

L. Fairfax.

Mike handed the letter to Linda and regarded Sanders with a speculative glint in his eye. 'Why did you bring this to me instead of showing it to Inspector Rodgers?'

'The man's obtuse, I told you. He'd either ignore it or accuse me of writing it myself.'

'Did you write it, Mr Sanders?'

Sanders let out a huge sigh of impatience and frustration. Picking up his hat and suede gloves he said, 'I'll leave the letter with you, Baxter. If it's important – and I think it is – you'll know how to cope with the situation. I'm expecting action from you, not the useless sort of evasions and inactivity one gets from the police. Now, if you'll excuse me, I have another appointment. You know my address, and the number's in the phone book if you should need to contact me. Good afternoon.'

When he had gone Mike grinned at Linda, whose lips were compressed in annoyance. 'Darling! Why on *earth* did you stand for it?' she demanded.

'Stand for what, darling?'

'He treated us like a couple of greenhorn recruits on the

barrack square. I swear that is the most arrogant man I have ever met in a whole lifetime. Why on earth didn't you throw him out?'

'The temptation was strong, I assure you. But I was intrigued to watch just how far his self-assurance stretched.'

'Until the crack of doom, I should think,' Linda said. 'Do you realise he hardly let you finish one sentence?'

'Yes, and I found that interesting. You see, he didn't come here to listen to me. That wasn't the point of the visit.'

'Then what was?'

'Sanders put me in mind of a sort of actor who has a nice little dramatic scene specially designed to give the play a lift. He even had a little piece of "stage business" to perform during his act – he had to deliver that letter. Have you had time to read it?'

'Yes, but it baffles me. What's this bit about a missing shoe?'

'That's a fact. There was a shoe missing when they found Lucy Staines's body. John Goldway confirmed it this morning.'

'It's rather a strange coincidence that we couldn't find one of Peggy Bedford's shoes when they took her away just now.'

Mike nodded. 'I'm curious to know just what Fairfax is getting at when he writes "I wonder whether you really did murder Lucy Staines? . . . I wonder if you just happened to be the unlucky one they've picked on." Whom do you suppose he means by "they"?'

'The police, or the Crown, surely?'

'Possibly. Or someone else. A gang, a group of some sort. In other words, Fairfax might be hinting that Weldon was framed.' Noting Linda's look of incredulity he went on, 'Stranger things than that have been known. Anyway, this letter appears to have put the lid on my interesting little theory about a Lord Fairfax hostelry. Mix some martinis, darling – not too heavy on the Noilly Prat.'

Linda nodded and said, 'I'll ask Mrs Potter for some ice.' She was interrupted by the telephone ringing, and lifted the receiver, then beckoned to her husband. 'It's Inspector Rodgers from Scotland Yard.'

'Hello, Inspector,' Mike said. 'I was just thinking about giving you a ring.'

'I'm afraid there's no news yet,' came Rodgers's matter-of-fact voice. 'The hospital's not very informative but I gather it's touch and go with the Bedford girl. I'll contact you the moment I hear something definite. That's not why I rang: we've traced that pub of yours, the Lord Fairfax.'

Mike ignored the sarcastic note in his voice and politely asked for details.

'It's in a quiet little village about six miles from Farnham out along the Hog's Back. Place called Westerdale.'

'Westerdale. Thanks very much, Inspector.'

'Will you be going down there?'

'Yes, I rather think I will, if that's all right by you?'

'Certainly. Saves me a journey. I'd come myself but I'm up to my neck in this new case at the Elephant. Keep me in the picture, will you, if anything interesting crops up?'

'Many thanks for calling, Inspector. Good night.'

Mike hung up and smiled at his wife. 'Well, we've started to make some progress. Half an hour ago we didn't have a single Fairfax, now we've got two: a man in Como and a pub near Farnham.'

'Which is first on our visiting list? . . . As if I didn't know!' said Linda sarcastically, putting away the gin and vermouth bottles with a show of heavy resignation.

Mike coughed apologetically. 'Yes . . . quite . . . I see what you mean . . . But Westerdale is a little more handy, don't you think, darling? Ask Mrs Potter to fix us a cold meal first; then I'll bring the car round.'

'Why don't we leave right away?'

'No, preferably after the evening rush-hour is over. There are a couple of decent stretches of road where I can see what sort of a job the garage has done on the car. There's nothing like a nice little spin in the country after a hard day's work in Town.'

Linda made a rude face and went to find Mrs Potter.

Later that evening as they set off Mike puzzled his wife by first driving to New Cavendish Street instead of taking the direct south-westerly route towards Surrey.

As he pulled in at the kerb Linda asked, 'Are we calling on that arrogant gent? If so, count me out.'

'No need for you to come up, darling. Get yourself a paper and mind the car. I'll only be a minute if Sanders is at home.'

Linda bought an evening paper and glanced at it with no great interest until she suddenly caught sight of a front-page story headline: FASHION MODEL ATTEMPTS SUICIDE. Beneath a photograph of Peggy Bedford was a brief account of how she had been found in a gas-filled room of a luxury flat near Baker Street that afternoon. Anxiously Linda scanned the short column for fear their names had been mentioned, but was relieved to find that Rodgers had kept his promise and protected them from unnecessary publicity. It was the surly porter who emerged as the hero of the day; by the time an imaginative journalist had finished with him he was a veritable giant who had broken into the locked door with one heave of his massive shoulders and had subsequently carried out heroic attempts at first aid.

Linda smiled and flicked idly through the remaining pages. The international crisis was still spluttering and she was just getting interested in the latest tit-bits concerning the TV star's missing poodle when Mike came out of Sanders's flat carrying a fairly large envelope.

'Got it!' he announced as he slid beside her and started up the throaty engine.

'Got what?'

'A good photograph of Lucy Staines. It was in a frame by Weldon's bedside. Thought there might be something like that available. That pompous ass Sanders refused to let me have it with the frame, so I slipped it out of the frame when he wasn't looking. It should help us if we're going to track down the girl's connection with the Lord Fairfax pub. Now then, let's see what the car can do if we're kind to her.'

Miraculously they reached Farnham without the clangour of a speed cop's bell in their ears, and then began studying the map for the tiny village of Westerdale. Darkness had fallen on the warm summer's evening as they completed the last part of their journey and now, in the dark, sparsely populated country lanes around the Hog's Back district they experienced some difficulty in finding the village.

'If it's as hard as this to find Westerdale, heaven knows how elusive the pub will be,' Mike observed.

The Lord Fairfax, when at last they ran it to earth, proved to be little more than a single room in which saloon and public bar were combined, an open fireplace festooned with horse-brasses, and a very large landlord. Two bright little eyes, like marbles swimming in oil, encased in rolls of unhealthy fat, flickered at them with unabashed curiosity as they entered, but the greeting was friendly enough.

'Evening, madam. Evening, sir. What'll you have?'

'Good evening. Gin and tonic, please.'

'With pleasure, sir. Two, will it be?'

'Make it three, if you'll join us?'

'Pleasure, sir, great pleasure.'

Mike joined Linda at a table by the window.

As the landlord busied himself behind the bar with their drinks he called out to them, 'Nice car you've got there, sir, if I may say so. Always did fancy a steel-blue Jag, if I ever came into the money. Come a long way, have you, sir? From London, perhaps?'

'As a matter of fact you're right, we have.'

'Thought so. Happened to be out in the yard when you pulled up. Noticed the engine was hot and the tyres pretty warm too.'

Linda pretended to drop her lighter and bent to pick it up. 'He doesn't miss much, does he?' she murmured.

'Yes . . . The name's Turner, by the way – Johnny Turner,' the landlord said hopefully as he poured three careful measures of gin and began slicing a lemon. 'In case you didn't see it over the door.'

'Nice to make your acquaintance, Mr Turner. I'm Mike Baxter. This is my wife, Linda.'

The two marbles gleamed with vivid interest. 'Not *the* Mike Baxter, the chap who writes all those newspaper articles?'

'Yes, I write for a living.'

'And a very nice living too, I'll bet. I'm a great fan of yours. I always read your articles. This is a pleasure, an honour indeed. Not often we get celebrities at a quiet place like this. I hope you'll do me the honour of taking a drink on the house.'

He rolled towards them with an eager smile, three glasses and three small tonics balanced on a tray. Mutual greetings were exchanged as they raised their glasses.

Turner launched into a lengthy account of the last occasion when a famous author happened to visit the Lord Fairfax. With a sly leer he ended, 'He said he was looking for a suitable background to one of his stories, a setting like this, quiet and off the beaten track.'

'Well, we're not looking for a setting, Mr Turner, but we would like to tax your memory for a moment, if you don't mind,' Mike replied, producing the envelope containing Lucy Staines's photograph. 'Tell me, have you ever seen this girl at the Fairfax?'

They watched him intently as his beady eyes examined the photograph. A gleam of recognition flickered for a moment, but there was genuine regret in his voice as he returned the photograph and said, 'It's Lucy Staines, isn't it?'

'You mean you know her?' Linda cried out.

Turner shook his head gloomily. 'Not personally. She's never been here, I'll stake my life on it.'

'Then how—'

'Her face was plastered all over the papers at the time of the murder trial. On the telly too. I'd know sure as eggs are eggs if she'd ever been here. They're going to hang the bloke that done it any day now, aren't they?'

Mike nodded grimly and drained his glass. It had been a long journey for nothing, and now they were going to have to sit for the sake of politeness through a second round of drinks which Turner, who was obviously starved of company, insisted on offering. The irony of it was, with a man of Turner's all-consuming curiosity and talent for observation, had Lucy Staines ever been within a mile of the Lord Fairfax those two sharp marble eyes would undoubtedly have spotted her.

Despondency set in and they let Turner do all the talking, until they felt they could decently leave. The landlord was clearly reluctant to let them go, and accompanied them to the door with much hand-shaking and good wishes for their return journey.

In their car Mike switched on the ignition and listened to the engine purring, and was just about to let in the clutch when Linda nudged him, indicating the rear mirror. They saw Turner waddling towards them, waving a newspaper in his hand.

'Tell him he can keep it,' said Linda as Mike put his head out of the window

'It's all right, old chap – thanks all the same. We'll get another back in Town,' Mike called out.

Turner shook his head, struggling for breath, his great frame shaking like jelly. 'That's not . . . what I was . . . running after you for. It's this picture here – look!'

He opened the newspaper and stabbed a fat finger at the story of Peggy Bedford's alleged suicide attempt. 'I've had *that* little number at the Fairfax all right,' he informed them.

'She was here? Are you quite sure?' Linda asked excitedly.

'No doubt about it at all. She was here at least three times this summer. I *thought* you might be interested, seeing as how it says she works at the same place as the murdered Staines girl. Look, it says here . . . "It is believed the two were close friends." That's why I ran after you before you drove off.'

'You have a good memory, Mr Turner,' said Mike. 'Can you remember anything about her – what she was wearing, what she drank, who she was with, and so on?'

'What she was wearing?' repeated Turner in an effort to remember. 'About as little as possible, I'd say. What she drank? Pink gins, like they was tap-water. I've seen some of 'em pour it down in my time, but she was way up on the list. Who was she with? Always the same bloke. Didn't look her type at all. Poker-faced sort of gent, quiet dresser, grey-haired, old enough to be her Dad. Reckon that's what he was too – her sugar-daddy. Walked with a bit of a limp, needed a stick he did. Not her type at all, I remember thinking.'

He winked at Linda and rubbed his hands. Mr Turner was obviously enjoying himself.

Chapter Four

Linda was the first to speak as they swung out on to the Hog's Back and headed for Guildford.

'As Mine Host with the elephantine memory so aptly put it, not her type at all. What on earth do you suppose old Staines was up to – living it up with someone scarcely old enough to be his daughter?'

'But the whole thing's impossible. *He* was the one who drew our attention in the first place to the Lord Fairfax. If he knew the significance of the entry in his daughter's diary why send me on this wild-goose chase? It just doesn't add up. Turner has probably got his wires crossed, though I must say those beady little eyes of his struck me as being phenomenally accurate. I swear he'll remember what shade of lipstick you used today if we go back in a year's time.'

Linda laughed. 'He probably will. But not so fast in dismissing Staines from the picture, darling. Do you remember his curious embarrassment when he had to bring out the name Peggy Bedford – almost as if it were a name never mentioned in polite company? I commented on it at the time, if you remember. Secondly, what was the address on his business card, the one with the name of the refrigerator firm on it?'

Mike thought for a second, then replied, 'Keane Brothers, Guildford. You're right! That's only a few miles from here. Therefore it's not out of the question that Staines should find his way to Westerdale; it's also a remote enough village if he was seeking a bit of privacy – look at the trouble we had finding it. But it still doesn't add up. Staines went out of his way to draw my attention to that diary entry; he's the one who started all this.'

Linda was silent for a while, then she asked, 'Mike, you remember the hotel where we had lunch with the Battsons last month?'

'Yes, the White Hart, wasn't it?'

'No, it was called the White Angel. What's the name of the inn near Hammersmith Bridge we sometimes visit on our walks by the river?'

'Darned if I know. But I don't quite see—'

'You had a drink with John last week, in Whitehall you told me. Which pub was it?'

'Darling, I don't gape at inn signs every time . . . Oh, I see what you're getting at! Maybe you have a point there.'

'I'm darn sure I have. Unless you are a confirmed pubcrawler or a collector of ancient inn signs I don't think more than one person in ten actually looks at the *name* of a pub before going inside it.'

'Brilliant, so far. But where does it get us? There are fifty-seven different varieties of reasons why Staines should be enjoying the company of a Bond Street model – the sugar-daddy angle sticks out a mile, but don't forget Peggy was a friend of his daughter's. It's not so unnatural after all.'

'Mike, sometimes you're too charitable to be real. I'm quite sure I've got Miss Peggy Bedford weighed up properly – call it feminine instinct. Anyway, now that we've found the Fairfax pub, with all its interesting associations, maybe there's also some implication in the Fairfax letter that has escaped us so far.'

'One might be forgiven for suspecting that it's a fake.'

Linda laughed. 'You *are* in a cautious mood tonight, aren't you, darling? Assuming one might be forgiven for assuming it might be a fake, what might one assume was the reason for Sanders coming to see you?'

Mike shook his head in bewilderment. After a while he ventured, 'Perhaps he's cut from the same cloth as Staines – his conscience is driving him to take action on Harold Weldon's behalf, but his private life won't allow of too close an inspection, especially by the police. I don't know, Linda darling, I just don't know at this stage of things. But I shall certainly spend a little time probing into the private lives of both those gentlemen. Maybe Harold Weldon will be able to enlighten us. He must have known them both pretty well. John Goldway's arranged for me to go down to Pentonville tomorrow morning.'

Linda shuddered dramatically. 'That's one little trip you can count me out on . . . I mean of.'

'Your grammar is appalling, and anyway you haven't been invited,' said Mike with a chuckle. 'Woman's place is in the home.'

Linda's retort was brief but forcible.

Before leaving for the prison the following morning Mike decided to telephone Hector Staines. He dialled the Guildford number and Keane Brothers referred him to a London exchange. Staines, it seemed, looked after the City end of the firm and lived in Bayswater.

When Staines's voice came on the line it was not quite as

clipped and impersonal as Mike remembered it. Though the elderly man was obviously trying to hide his emotions Mike's sharp ear caught some hint of inner turmoil. He was not long in finding the cause.

'I've been to the hospital this morning, Baxter. They won't let me talk to P . . . to Miss Bedford. It's terrible.'

'Is she still unconscious?'

'Yes. What a shocking business! I can't imagine what could have possessed her to do such a thing. She was always so full of the joy of living.'

'So I gather, Mr Staines. Tell me, she was a good friend not only of your daughter but of yourself, wasn't she?'

'What's that you're saying? Peggy . . . Miss Bedford a friend of mine? That's an exaggeration. I've hardly met her more than a handful of times.'

'When was the last time you took her to the Lord Fairfax?' Mike demanded bluntly.

There was an awkward pause. Staines's voice, when it came, was weak and high-pitched. 'The Lord what? I'm afraid I don't know what you're talking about.'

'Is that possible, Mr Staines? The Lord Fairfax is a little pub not far from Farnham: horse-brasses round the open fireplace, plus a landlord with gimlet eyes. The village is called Westerdale.'

'Oh. I see. That's the pub you mean. I . . . I had no idea of the name of the place. The Lord Fairfax, you say? How extraordinary!'

'Yes, isn't it? Now perhaps you'll tell me whom your daughter had planned to meet there at eight-thirty on May 12th. You'll hardly have forgotten the entry in her diary.'

'Good gracious! This is news to me. I don't understand it at all.'

'But you admit to taking Peggy to the Fairfax?'

'My dear fellow, I admit – as you somewhat crudely put it – having been to Westerdale once—'

'Once? Or several times?'

'I do wish you'd stop badgering me; it is quite unnecessary. I just did not notice what the pub was called. As a matter of fact it was not I who took Peggy, but the other way round – she took *me* there. I just happened to bump into her one day in Farnham. She was delivering a dress to some . . . er . . . clients. My head office is in Guildford, that's how I happened to be in the neighbourhood. I have to go down there about once a week.' He paused, then added earnestly, 'It was quite a chance meeting.'

It sounded a skilful mixture of the truth and some rather lame prevarication but Mike decided not to press the point.

Staines went on, 'I must say, I fail to understand why Peggy didn't spot the significance of the Fairfax entry in Lucy's diary.'

'Did you show it to her?'

'Of course I did, shortly before the trial came on. She said it meant nothing to her at all.'

Miss Peggy Bedford could very well have been lying, Mike thought. It seemed likely that it was she who had arranged to meet Lucy Staines at the Westerdale pub shortly before the latter was murdered. What the meeting was to be about, and why the Bedford girl had lied, was something Mike could only guess at. Feeling that there was little more to be extracted from this conversation Mike rang off and was just about to leave when the phone rang.

It was Inspector Rodgers. As usual, he did not waste his words. 'The hospital has just informed me that Peggy Bedford has died!'

'Oh no! The poor kid. Did she regain consciousness at all?'

'I'm afraid not. Wish she had; there were a few questions we would have liked to put to her.'

'Yes. I had some myself. By the way, Inspector, about the missing shoe – has it turned up yet?'

'No. But we'll find it, don't worry,' Rodgers answered curtly and hung up.

There can be few more depressing places on earth than Her Majesty's Prison at Pentonville. Mike found himself shivering as the warder led him along echoing corridors of concrete and steel to his meeting with Harold Weldon.

'How is he?' Mike asked quietly as they approached the cell.

'Weldon? He's behaving rather well, sir, considering the circumstances. He's been doing a lot of reading. Can't understand half the books he asks for, myself, but they seem to keep him quiet. Funnily enough, we don't get a lot of trouble with them, not at this stage.'

The warder produced a large key and unlocked the door.

'You've got a visitor, Mr Weldon,' he announced.

Mike's immediate and somewhat distorted impression was of a hermit. A thin, bony, lanky hermit with a long, slightly twisted nose, lifeless hair that hung long and partly screened a pair of hostile grey eyes.

'If you're another parson you can bloody well go back to your pulpit!' The voice was nasal, cultured, and devoid of any wish to charm.

'I'm not a clergyman,' Mike replied equably. 'My name is Mike Baxter. I'm a personal friend of Superintendent Goldway and Inspector Rodgers.'

'How cosy for you. You mix in very select circles. Had they been friends of mine I might not be here. What do you want?'

'I'd like to talk to you.'

'Why?' The prisoner had risen and now leant with his arms folded, propping himself up in one corner of the cell and eyeing Mike with undisguised suspicion and dislike. Suddenly he added, 'What did you say your name was?'

'Mike Baxter.'

'The journalist?'

'Yes.'

'Ah! I get it.' His pale eyes glinted maliciously and the incipient sneer grew to a king-size expression of contempt. 'Snooping around for a little first-hand copy, eh? It'll all be in your next neat little article, won't it? The raving beast in the padded cell, death's imprint clearly legible in his sunken eyes. Well, I'll do a little raving for you, so as not to disappoint your public. How do you want it, penny plain or tuppence—'

'You're wasting my time,' Mike snapped.

Something in his tone brought Weldon to a dead stop.

Mike continued in a crisp voice, 'Two questions for you, then you can go back to hamming it up. Did you murder Lucy Staines?'

Weldon's lip curled sardonically and he gave a laugh. 'Don't you bother to read the newspapers? Of course I murdered Lucy. It was my Freudian way of proving my love for her. I lost my temper in a public place of entertainment, so that everyone could see us, persuaded her to come with me to a nice deserted demolition-site, sat around for an hour or two till the ghoulish chimes of midnight sounded, strangled her, acquired a sample of her blood as a chilly sort of memento; it was all quite simple, nothing complicated about it. A red-headed hag named Nadia Tarrant saw me do it, or at least saw me running noisily out of Soho Square. I wore special hob-nailed boots so she couldn't possibly miss me.'

'But she *did* spot you, didn't she? At the identification parade the next day?'

Weldon's voice dropped to a contemptuous snarl as he replied, 'If you paid that old trout enough money she'd swear her own grandmother was Brigitte Bardot.'

'Anything else?' asked Mike patiently.

'Let me see, what did I do next? Ah yes, just to seal matters nicely, I hadn't an alibi, the blood-group checked, and I made two statements to the gentlemen of the Law, both highly contradictory and highly implausible. So there you have it. As one of your literary confrères put it with such startling originality – "an open-and-shut case".'

'I see.'

'Have we had Question Number Two yet? My time is limited too,' said Weldon with an ironic sneer. 'Nine days and a handful of hours, to be precise.'

'I'm sorry,' Mike murmured, though he was not quite sure exactly what he was apologising for. 'The other question is simpler. Did you steal Lucy Staines's shoe?'

Weldon turned his back on him and laughed again. 'The missing shoe! What fun the Press had with that!'

He swung round, contempt and truculence again dominating his pale features. 'Of course I stole it. I'm a collector of women's shoes. I've got cupboards full of 'em at home.' He pretended a look of stupid cunning and came close to Mike. 'You're not a collector too, by any chance? I'd love to show you some of my prize exhibits – maybe we could do some swapping?'

'For Pete's sake cut out the clowning! Did you steal her shoe?'

'I keep telling you I did.'

'Why?'

'One doesn't commit a murder every day, chum. It was quite an occasion. I took the shoe as a souvenir.'

'Left or right?'

'Come again?'

'Only one shoe was missing. Which did you take, the left or the right one?'

There was a moment's pause in Weldon's truculence. He pursed his lips, shrugged his shoulders, and said, 'The left.'

'Wrong!' snapped Mike.

'Really?'

'It was the right shoe that was missing.'

'You don't tell me?'

Mike busied himself with lighting a cigarette, which he offered to the prisoner. Weldon shook his head contemptuously. The exchange over the shoe had gone rapidly, but Mike had been watching his man's every reaction. Weldon's complete indifference of tone was of a quality no guilty man could possibly have assumed. Conviction surged inside him: the only thing Weldon was guilty of was bad luck and a maddening talent for getting people's backs up.

Mike said urgently, 'Weldon, listen to me, and for God's sake listen carefully. We've not got much time, neither you nor I. If *you* have only got nine days and a handful of hours till . . .'

'I hang by the neck until I be dead.'

'—then *I've* only got the same amount of time to try and help you.'

'That's the bit that puzzles me,' Weldon cut in. 'Why *do*

you want to help me? Surely that smarmy dago Mainardi didn't send you? I'll bet he hasn't given me a single thought, except to wonder when his fat fee will be paid.'

'You must have second sight.'

'So you *have* been to see him?'

'Yes.'

'What did you think of him?'

'I was not impressed.'

'Strike one for you, Baxter. Maybe I should have hired you to defend me.'

'I'm not a lawyer.'

'No, you're not. Just a very successful journalist.'

'I'm not proposing to write a single line about you, Weldon. I'd genuinely like to help you, that's my sole reason for coming here. There's only one way to save your neck and that's to find out who did murder Lucy Staines. Do *you* have any idea?'

Weldon shrugged his shoulders, but he was calmer now. 'None whatsoever. Naturally I've given the matter some thought – what the devil was she doing in Soho Square at that time of night, and so on? The only answer that adds up is that it was one of those senseless crimes committed by some faceless ghoul with no motive whatsoever, not even robbery or sex.'

Mike shook his head. 'I don't believe in faceless killers or crimes without a motive. If I'm going to crack this case I've got to get hold of some facts. I can't make bricks without straw, and right now the only two wisps of straw I have are Hector Staines and Victor Sanders.'

Weldon stared at him incredulously. 'You don't mean to tell me you list *them* as suspects? You're nuts!'

'Possibly. If they aren't suspects I'm damned sure they're

both concealing something. And Peggy Bedford too – only I moved too slowly there.'

'What do you mean? Has something happened to Peggy?' He looked mildly concerned, but there was no other emotion to be read in his eyes.

'Yes. She committed suicide yesterday. Plugged up all the doors and windows of her flat and turned on the gas taps.'

Weldon suddenly dug his finger-nails into the palms of his hands until the white of his knuckles showed. 'That's terrible,' he muttered. 'Are you quite sure you've got your facts right?'

'Yes. Why?'

'It's only that . . . well, Peggy never struck me as the morbid type. Very much the contrary. She got a kick out of life, whatever else one may have thought about her.'

Mike raised his eyebrows questioningly.

Weldon continued, 'In a way I'm not too surprised she came to a sticky end, but I would never have thought it would be by her own hand.'

'Are you suggesting someone murdered her too?'

Weldon frowned. 'I know nothing about the circumstances of her death, other than what you've told me. But I wouldn't rule it out entirely.'

Mike digested this for several moments, then said, 'You must be sick of doing this, but would you care to give me a straightforward account of what really happened the night your fiancée was killed?'

Weldon sighed wearily and thrust the lank hair out of his eyes. 'Here we go again, once more round the Wrekin. However, if you think it'll do any good . . . Lucy and I had a row, she left me outside the theatre, and I walked down to the car park. I drove around for about an hour and then I put the car in St James's Square and went for a walk.'

'Why?'

'Because I was upset about the quarrel, about the things I'd said in the heat of the moment to Lucy. I wanted to cool off, to do a little straight thinking about our coming marriage. I walked a long way, as far as the Victoria and Albert Museum, then I retraced my steps, picked up the car, and drove home. I got back about half-past twelve.'

Mike looked at him and shrugged. 'It's not a very good alibi, is it?'

'It was never meant as an alibi. If I'd wanted one I'd have thought up something very much better than that.'

'You did.'

'Come again?'

'In your first statement to the police you told them you arrived home at half-past ten.'

'Ah yes. Silly of me, really. I suppose I lost my head. The news that she'd been strangled put me into a flat spin.'

'I see. What about this Tarrant woman? When she picked you out at the line-up had *you* ever seen *her* before?'

'No, thank you. I've never been a fan of vaudeville. Above my head.'

'Why vaudeville?'

'You haven't done your homework, Baxter. Nadia Tarrant was the hind legs of a horse, or part of a juggling act – I forget which. It came out at the trial. She was so hard up for a job on the boards she'd have sworn—'

'I know: that Brigitte Bardot was her grandmother! All right. It might be worth my while taking a crack at her just as soon as I can. Another question: did you ever visit a pub called the Lord Fairfax, or plan or arrange to do so?'

'Man alive, I've been in thousands of pubs in my time! Do you expect me to remember every one of 'em?'

'No. But does the Lord Fairfax ring a bell?'

Weldon shook his head thoughtfully. 'No bells.'

'Or perhaps a person called L. Fairfax?'

'No bells again . . . Wait . . . wasn't there a name like that in Lucy's diary?'

'Yes. But you say you'd never heard it before it was brought up at the trial?'

'Never.'

Mike took out his wallet and extracted the letter which Victor Sanders had brought him. 'Read this and tell me what you think of it.'

Weldon read the letter swiftly, then once more with care. Then he scowled and tossed it carelessly back into Mike's lap.

'Another bird with missing shoes on the brain. But the letter's addressed to me; how did you get hold of it?'

'Your friend Sanders opened it and brought it to me.'

Weldon gave a thin chuckle. 'Victor is a sport but he's wasting his time. This thing wouldn't fool the village idiot.'

'You think it's a fake?'

'Of course. Don't you?'

'Possibly. But that still leaves the question open as to why Sanders should have bothered to concoct it, assuming he did.'

'The answer's obvious, I should say. He's a dear old buffer, even if a bit dense. He's simply trying to help me.'

'How?'

'By stirring up some interest. After all, he's aroused yours, hasn't he? Strike one for Victor.'

'Yes,' Mike acknowledged cautiously, 'but it was actually Hector Staines who first pulled me into this. What were your relations with him?'

'My prospective dad-in-law that was? Oh, we got along. Rather a stuffed shirt of the old school. We had some hellish rows about design, sometimes. He seems to think architecture reached its peak with the Albert Memorial. But he's a decent enough old bird.'

'What about his sex life?' Mike shot at him bluntly. 'Does he incline towards young girls?'

'Who – old Hector?' Weldon seemed amused. 'I don't think he knows the difference between a woman and a refrigerator. He's been a widower for over twenty years – pillar of the church, pillar of local society, pillar of just about everything, I should say.'

'Isn't that the type who all too often—?'

Weldon waved aside the idea. 'No, no, you're on the wrong track there, chum. Hector's only failing is that he's always chronically hard up. No talent for making money whatsoever. But a good stick all the same.'

'I see.' Mike moved towards the door. 'I'll come down again soon, just as soon as I've got my hands on something concrete,' he promised.

'Try the Tarrant woman,' advised Weldon. 'See if you can persuade her to stop acting and tell the truth.'

'I intend to. Now listen, Weldon: if Superintendent Goldway or Inspector Rodgers come to see you – or anyone else for that matter – don't lose your temper, and don't get facetious. Do you understand? I can't promise you anything positive, but you'll certainly get negative results if you insist on antagonising people who want to help.'

'I'll study my Dale Carnegie assiduously every night, Daddy-o!'

'You could do worse.'

The two men shook hands and Mike turned to leave. At

the door he said carelessly over one shoulder, 'And by the way, if they ask you again about Lucy's missing shoe, keep quiet and say nothing. Your guesses are too good.'

'How do you mean?'

'It *was* the left shoe that was missing.'

Chapter Five

Mike Baxter was only a trifle late for his luncheon appointment with Superintendent Goldway. Goldway listened in noncommittal silence as Mike described his interview with Harold Weldon.

'You understand, John, I'm not very smitten with Weldon as a man, but I'm pretty well convinced that he didn't murder Lucy Staines. In the first place he's far too intelligent a type not to have thought up a more effective alibi, had he strangled her in a moment of passion.'

'You're on thin ice there, Mike,' Goldway interrupted. 'Premeditated crime and crimes of passion call for two different types of alibi. The Crown maintained that it was just because he *did* lose his head, and his temper, followed by the strangling, that he *did* have such a weak alibi.'

Mike shook his head stubbornly. 'Maybe he's the type to do irrational things at moments of passion – but by the time the police hauled him in the next day he'd have cooled off and have thought up something better; he had plenty of time. No, my money is on Weldon's innocence, however awkward a cuss he may be. Look at that trap I set him concerning the missing shoe. He hadn't the faintest idea which shoe had been taken. If he'd contradicted me when I told him the wrong one then I'd have caught him on the hop. But he hadn't a clue, and furthermore he wasn't the least bit interested.'

'I ought to trust your judgement, Mike – you've been right often enough before,' said Goldway with a twinkle in his eyes. 'But this time I really think you're heading down the wrong track. The evidence against Weldon was overwhelming. Even if I wanted to, I very much doubt if there is any way I could help you. The case is officially closed.'

'It's not closed for me until five minutes before they hang Weldon.'

'That gives you exactly nine days. You'll have to get a move on!'

'I know.' He put his napkin to one side and rose from the table. 'Forgive me if I skip the dessert. Were you able to get me the Tarrant woman's address?'

Goldway nodded and delved into one waistcoat pocket, producing a slip of paper. 'I could probably start an unofficial probe on her if it's any help,' he offered.

'No, let me have a go on my own first. If I need help I'll contact you and then we can increase the pressure,' decided Mike. 'Thank you for an excellent lunch. Goodbye, John.'

Mike left the club and drove to a coffee-bar where he had arranged to meet Linda. When he found her table he did not sit down.

'Haven't you time for a coffee, darling?' she asked.

'I'm afraid not. I'll tell you all about my morning on our way to this Tarrant woman.'

As they drove through the thick swirl of traffic in Trafalgar Square he gave Linda a condensed account of his impressions of Harold Weldon and of his luncheon with the Superintendent.

'John's hands are tied, of course, I appreciate that. But he let me read between the lines: he'll help us on the quiet if we really do stumble across anything significant.'

Linda nodded. 'He's a dear, even if he is aiding and abetting in the postponement of my holiday! Incidentally, speaking of stumbling across something significant, I saw our mutual friend the red-faced colonel at lunch today.'

'Sanders? What was so significant about that?'

'The company he was in.'

'Male or female?'

'Female.'

'Good for old Victor! Didn't know he was so human. I hope he was enjoying himself.'

'That's just it – I don't think he was. A woman can tell instinctively whether it's the male or the female who's making all the moves. Sanders looked positively uncomfortable.'

Mike laughed. 'Too bad for him. What's his taste like?'

'I don't need to describe her, just tell you who she is.'

'The suspense is killing me.'

'Irene Long,' said Linda laconically.

'Who?' Mike swerved sharply to snap up a place in the next lane and prepared for a right turn towards Soho Square. 'Who the heck's Irene Long?'

'Darling! Mind that cyclist, I'm sure he wants to live . . . You don't remember Irene Long? She's at Conway and Racy's – the one who looked after my suit and sold me that darling little hat.'

'Oh, *that* female. The blonde with all the make-up and the terribly arch smile?'

'None other.'

'How very interesting. They must have made an odd couple.'

Linda smiled. 'So you see? I thought you'd be happy to have something to think about.'

Mike smiled and answered dryly, 'I have so little on my mind . . .'

Turning the car into the Square he drove close to the kerb and peered at the numbers of the buildings. 'It must be somewhere on this side.'

After a short while they found the number they were looking for and by a stroke of luck were able to park the car quite near.

Linda got out and gazed dubiously at the grimy building, wrinkling her nose. 'Are you sure this is right, darling? It looks all offices to me. Surely no one actually lives here?'

'Not necessarily – this type of place generally has a few dingy back rooms let off as digs. Nadia Tarrant used to be the hind legs in a vaudeville horse or something, so I don't suppose she can afford to live in a palace.'

Linda discovered a rust-covered bell-push beside a scrap of dirty pasteboard with some near-indecipherable writing on it. 'I think this is it,' she said.

'Press it and we'll soon find out.'

Linda did so, but no sound came from within. She tried again but there was no answering peal. 'I'd have been surprised if it *had* worked.'

Mike grunted. 'The lift's out of order too. We'll have to walk up.'

They climbed three flights of filthy stairs, and then they came to a door with paint peeling off it, slightly ajar. A more recent square of pasteboard bore the neat lettering: NADIA TARRANT, VARIETY ARTISTE.

There was no bell or knocker. They were startled by the sudden shrill ringing of a telephone from the other side of the door. No one seemed to be in any hurry to answer it. Mike shrugged his shoulders and rapped two or three times with his knuckles without reply. They waited in silence as the telephone ceased to ring. He knocked again with his fist, felt the door give, and pushed it open.

The combined odours of stale bedding, spilt cocoa near a two-ring gas cooker, and humid washing hung out to dry over a sink stacked with greasy crockery assailed them. At first glance it appeared to be a typical sleazy bed-sitting room occupied by an uncommonly untidy woman.

Mike glanced round the room and his eye was immediately caught by a number of faded photographs and theatre bills plastered on the walls, evidently relics of Miss Tarrant's career in vaudeville. Judging by the photographs it was some years since their subject had been seen on the stage. It was hard to tell which of the nebulous, badly printed figures might be Nadia Tarrant, though one large, tinted photograph of a big bosomed girl with red hair, dressed in spangles and black tights, caught his eye and put him in mind of the pre-war days when colour photography had hardly got into its stride. As he bent to examine it Linda said doubtfully, 'Darling, do you think we ought to prowl round like this?'

Mike's answer was cut off by the telephone's sudden ring. He stiffened, looked across at Linda, and said, 'Answer it, darling.'

She reached out a hand, then hesitated.

'Go on! I've got to get tabs on this woman somehow, it's worth the risk.'

'But, Mike, we can't—'

'We can. Pick it up and listen. Don't say who you are.'

Linda sighed, and nervously picked up the receiver.

The voice that came booming over the line was instantly recognisable. 'Is that Gerrard 7311?'

'Yes.'

'Is that Nadia Tarrant?' came the stern, resonant voice of Victor Sanders again.

Linda looked questioningly at her husband, who rapidly motioned to her to carry on.

'Yes.'

'Why didn't you answer before? I telephoned five minutes ago. Are you trying to play tricks with me?'

'I was out,' Linda said in a rough voice, making a wild guess at the sort of tones Nadia Tarrant might use.

'Well, what about the Bannister affair? Do I get the third shoe?' Sanders barked. 'Hello . . . Are you listening?'

'Yes.'

'Speak up, woman. D'you understand me? I want that third shoe. And no monkey business!'

'Yes, all right.' There was a click of the replaced receiver at the other end.

Mike had put an ear to the receiver and listened to the strange dialogue.

Linda was shaking slightly and kept her hand on the phone as if to support herself.

'Victor Sanders,' she whispered. 'What on earth do you make of it, Mike? How does he come to be mixed up in this?' She glanced round the sordid room.

Mike nodded. 'Now he wants the third shoe,' he mused. 'What's behind all this I wonder?'

'What did he mean by "the Bannister affair"? Who is Bannister in this case?'

'I've never heard of him. You did splendidly, Linda. I wonder if Sanders recognised your voice?'

Linda started to answer, 'I tried to disguise it,' then broke off. 'Mike, there's someone coming up the stairs!'

They waited out of sight of the half-open door, which was suddenly pushed wide open. A big-bosomed woman in her late forties with flaming red hair of an impossible colour stood in the entrance, glaring angrily at them.

'Who are you? And what d'you want?' she said roughly.

Mike answered in a polite tone, 'Miss Nadia Tarrant?'

'Yes. Who gave you permission to barge in here like—?'

'The door was open, we—'

'I know the door was open. I left it on the catch. I've just nipped out to borrow something from a neighbour. What's the big idea, eh?'

'I apologise, Miss Tarrant, but we did ring the bell downstairs, and when there was no reply—'

'You just walked in! Well, you can just walk out, both of you! Go on, get out, before I send for the police!'

Linda made as if to leave but Mike restrained her. He leaned against the sink and returned the woman's aggressive glare with a smile. 'My name is Baxter – Mike Baxter. This is my wife. I'm a friend of Inspector Rodgers,' he announced.

'So what?'

'We just wanted to have a little chat, that's all.'

The woman stared at him suspiciously. 'You did, did you? Well, you're unlucky. I'm just off.'

'It won't take long, Miss Tarrant. Three or four minutes at the most.'

The woman hesitated, then looked at her wristwatch. 'Sorry, I can't oblige. I'm due at work at the café, and I'm late already.'

'What café? I thought you were on the stage.'

'I'm resting between engagements, if it's any of your

flaming business! I'll work where I want to – without asking your permission, Mr Flaming Nosy Parker!'

Mike apologised as politely as ever, then turning to Linda he said pleasantly, 'Come along, darling. We won't bother Miss Tarrant after all. I'll explain to Rodgers. It probably wasn't a good suggestion anyway.'

He brushed past her and walked out into the corridor.

'Wait a tick!' she called. He half turned and heard her say, 'I suppose I was a bit rude. But you shouldn't go barging in on people's private property like that. Specially when I haven't had a chance to tidy up. Now, what d'you want?'

Closing the door, Mike came back into the room. 'Just a very short chat about the Weldon case, that's all. But we don't want to make you late for your work.'

The woman made an ugly grimace. 'For creep's sake, the Weldon case again! Lord, am I sick and tired of that name!'

'Yes, I can well imagine. But you were an important witness, so I'm afraid it's inevitable—'

She drew herself up. 'Important! I was the *only* witness.'

'Quite. Tell me, Miss Tarrant, where are you working now?'

'At Farnalio's in Greek Street.'

'Were you coming back from Farnalio's the night you saw Weldon?'

'Yes.'

'It was just after twelve?'

'Are you asking me or telling me?' she snapped.

Mike smiled apologetically. 'I'm asking you.'

'Yes, it was soon after twelve. I saw him running off the demolition-site. He bumped into me.'

'You're sure it was Weldon?'

''Course I'm sure. Think I'd have stood up in the witness—'

'What was he wearing, do you remember?'

The woman hesitated for a second, then answered, 'No, I don't remember. Look, I've been through all this rigmarole a score of times already. I saw Weldon, and I told the coppers about it, and I picked him out at the line-up. What more d'you want?'

Linda unexpectedly interrupted them. 'You must have a very good memory for faces, unless of course you'd seen him before?'

The woman's eyes narrowed, as if she sensed a trap. 'What d'you mean?' she asked suspiciously.

'I only wondered if you might have met or seen Harold Weldon *before* he bumped into you that night.'

'Have a heart! As if I mix with that toffee-nosed lot! Of course I hadn't. Now look, I'm supposed to be at work by four, so if you don't mind—'

Mike nodded. 'Yes, of course. We won't keep you any longer. Oh, there is just one more point, though. When Weldon bumped into you, did he say anything?'

Again the hesitation, and the narrowed eyes searching for a trap. At length she muttered a gruff negative.

'Are you sure?' Mike pressed her.

'Well . . . if he did, I didn't hear him.'

'But I thought you told Inspector Rodgers that he *did* say something, only you couldn't understand what it was?'

'I . . . I don't remember exactly what I told the police.'

Mike smiled sweetly. 'No? Yet you've got a very good memory, Miss Tarrant.'

'I've got a very good memory for faces, and I shan't forget yours in a hurry, believe you me,' she snarled.

'I see. So, as far as you can remember, Weldon didn't say anything. He just pushed you on one side—'

She nodded reluctantly.

'But obviously you had a good look at him?'

'I identified him, didn't I? How could I identify him if I hadn't had a good look at him?'

'Quite. How could you?' Mike replied musingly.

Nadia Tarrant opened her mouth, changed her mind, and stood to one side so as to allow them access to the door. 'Now come on, I've got to get cracking and I want to lock up. You wouldn't like a key, would you, just in case you feel like dropping in at any time?'

Linda let out an exclamation, partly relief and partly embarrassment, as they came out into the Square and made for the car. 'Where exactly did that get us?'

'I'm not quite sure,' Mike replied. 'Two steps forward and one step back, I rather think. The Sanders business baffles me completely for the time being, but that revolting character up there would sell her own mother if someone paid her a fiver. Just as Weldon said.'

'If she ever had a mother,' Linda commented dryly as she got into the car. 'Where are we going now?'

Mike let in the clutch and drove off slowly, deep in thought. 'I must do some telephoning,' he decided. 'John promised to put some pressure on the Tarrant woman if I thought it necessary. And it's just possible we might crack this case sooner than we thought.'

'How?'

'By finding out who bribed her to pick out Harold Weldon at the identification parade. She probably had a good look at some photos of him before she trotted on to do her stuff.'

But twenty minutes later, on returning to their Eaton Square flat, Mike's optimism gradually faded. Inspector

Rodgers was waiting in the hall, chatting amiably to Mrs Potter. His manner became crisp and tense when the Baxters arrived, but they were both too buoyed up on their new wave of optimism to notice it immediately.

'I saw Weldon at Pentonville this morning, Inspector,' Mike announced.

Rodgers nodded. 'I know. The Superintendent mentioned it. What d'you make of him, Mr Baxter?'

'He's nobody's pin-up boy but I'm convinced he didn't murder his fiancée.'

The Inspector pursed his lips and made an obvious attempt to listen patiently. 'An interesting theory, Mr Baxter, but you'll hardly expect me to agree.'

Baxter related the incident of the missing shoe and the trap which he had set for the condemned man, then added his theories about Weldon's failure to invent for himself a more effective alibi.

Rodgers smiled sceptically. 'And that's all you've got to go on, Mr Baxter?'

'No, there's one bit more. We've just been visiting the witness – the *only* witness – who claimed to identify him. I'd like you to put that woman on the mat for a little tough questioning, if you will.' He paused expectantly.

The Inspector held up a warning hand. '*Who* do you think you've been visiting?'

'Nadia Tarrant, of course. In her bed-sitter in Soho Square.'

The Inspector shook his head sadly. 'Someone's been playing a vicious little game with you, I'm afraid. I've just come up from Surrey. There's been a fresh murder down there. God knows who fooled you at Soho Square but the woman we found in some woods a few miles from Farnham was unquestionably Nadia Tarrant. I identified her myself.'

'That's impossible!' Linda cried. 'We've just been talking to her. A tough type in her late forties, with dyed red hair. Haven't we, Mike?'

Mike crushed his unlit cigarette in his fingers and wearily shook his head. 'Darling, the Inspector headed the team who worked on the Weldon case. If he says he's seen the Tarrant witness dead in some Surrey woods, then that's where she is, not talking to us in Soho Square. We've been had!'

'By a remarkably good impersonation, it seems,' Rodgers put in rather smugly.

Mike shrugged his shoulders. 'Well, neither of us have actually ever seen her in person, you know. We weren't present at the trial.'

'That's true,' Rodgers said. 'Nevertheless, from Mrs Baxter's description it doesn't sound surprising that she took you in.' He stood up. 'I think I had better hurry down to Soho Square and bring this impostor in for questioning right away. Are you coming with me, Mr Baxter?'

'I will, if I may?'

'I'd be glad of your assistance in identifying her. Oh, there's one point I forgot to mention in regard to this Farnham murder. Whoever killed the real Nadia Tarrant took one of her shoes with him.'

Chapter Six

Inspector Rodgers's driver knew all the short cuts, and they lost little time getting back to Soho Square. It was clear at once, however, that they were too late. The bird had flown. She had had time enough to search for whatever she had come to find; the room looked as though a bulldozer had driven carelessly through it.

'I take it that it didn't look like this when you and your wife arrived?' the Inspector said grimly.

'Untidy, yes; but not like this,' Mike replied.

'I see. That means she hadn't had quite enough time to search for whatever she wanted when you surprised her.'

'You mean you think she was already in here?'

'It's a guess, but it adds up,' Rodgers said. 'The door was open, you told me. She must have heard you climbing the stairs. There's no carpet.'

'We must have heralded our approach pretty effectively,' agreed Mike.

'Exactly! She heard you coming, abandoned her search, slipped out into the corridor and hid just round the corner of the corridor, within earshot. She may even have gleaned from your conversation that you didn't actually know Nadia

Tarrant by sight. She must have wanted to get into that room urgently, so she decided to get rid of you by pretending to be Nadia Tarrant. Judging from the dyed hair and her knowledge of the Weldon case she's been keeping a close eye on Nadia Tarrant. She'd have fooled anybody who wasn't actually at the trial, and maybe quite a few who were.'

Mike nodded, feeling a trifle foolish that they had been duped, despite the Inspector's excuses on his behalf. Gazing round the disorderly room he said, 'I take it we'd better not touch anything?'

'Correct. There may be some useful fingerprints. Apart from the impersonation angle, it's a clear case of breaking and entering.' He strode to the telephone and put in a clipped, factual call to his office.

Mike lit a cigarette and offered his case to the Inspector. When the call was finished Mike said, 'I'd give my eye-teeth to know what she was looking for.'

Rodgers smiled thinly. 'I think we might take a guess at that. Probably a lady's shoe.'

Mike's eyebrows shot up. 'What makes you think that?'

'It seems to be part of the pattern, don't you think?'

After a moment's hesitation Mike decided to tell Rodgers about the telephone call Linda had taken from Victor Sanders. 'Sanders wanted to know when he was going to get hold of "the third shoe",' he concluded.

'He said that?' Rodgers murmured, rubbing his clipped brown hair with the palm of his hand, a habit of his when thinking deeply. Despite his physique he looked tired and worried. When Mike had finished he remarked, 'I've got two murder investigations on my hands at the moment – the one this morning at Farnham, and the Elephant and Castle stabbing – only it's not just a stabbing anymore, it's a murder.

You'll understand that I'm not looking for work and I'm in no hurry to reopen the Weldon case. But I have to admit there are one or two things that are beginning to make me think again. Sanders, for one. He struck me as a decent type, at the time of the trial, not the type to lie. Now I'm not so sure.'

'That makes two of us. Is he married?'

'No. But he's quite a ladies' man, I rather gathered. He has a splendid war record, DSO and one or two good medals, private income from property left him by his father—'

'But what does he do for a living?'

'Enjoys life, so far as I could ascertain. Spends his time travelling and dabbling in amateur photography. Not so amateur, either; I've seen some of his work, it's of quite a high standard.'

Mike was silent for a moment, then he asked, 'Whom do you suppose he was referring to when he mentioned the name Bannister? Was there anyone of that name mixed up in the case?'

Rodgers shook his head. 'No, not as far as I remember. I'll look into it.'

They both turned as they heard cautious footsteps advancing up the stone stairs. 'Some of your men?' Mike asked, but Rodgers motioned him to silence and murmured, 'No policeman ever walks as quietly as that.'

The footsteps paused at the landing, then advanced with obvious hesitation towards the partly open door. Mike and the Inspector kept very quiet and out of sight. There was a soft tap on the door. A young male voice with a marked accent called out, 'Nadia, *carissima*, it's me, Luigi. May I come in?'

Rodgers took a quick step and flung open the door. A

thin, pale-faced youth with thick, wavy, black hair and Latin features gazed fearfully at them for a second, then turned to run. Rodgers, moving with astonishing speed for one of his build, grabbed the youth by the jacket collar. With a jerk he spun the creature round and frog-marched him back into the room.

'Just where were you off to in such a hurry, my lad?'

The youth stammered something in Italian.

'You were coming in here, weren't you? What for?' persisted Rodgers.

'I wanted to see Nadia. Where is she?' He cast a dazed glance round the turmoil in the room. 'What has happened here? Has something . . . Is Nadia in trouble?'

'Sit down, laddie, and we'll have a little chat. I'm a police inspector. Now, what's your name, apart from Luigi? Supposing you tell me all about yourself?'

The youth sank on to the bed and darted frightened glances at them. Apparently drawing some reassurance from what he saw he began talking in a low voice.

'Luigi Saltoni. I am a waiter at Leonardo's Restaurant, near where Nadia works. My work permit is in order, I can show it to you if you wish.'

Rodgers smiled, his manner forbiddingly gentle, like a cat playing with a mouse. 'I'm very glad to hear it, Luigi. And I gather Miss Tarrant is a friend of yours, is she? We heard you call out *"carissima"* from the corridor there, so you needn't waste time pretending you're strangers. When did you last see her?'

'Last night. We had a meal at my rooms. I live in Meryl Street, you know, near Euston station. You've got to tell me, is something wrong?'

'Just let me ask the questions for the time being, Luigi.'

Bit by bit the Inspector extracted all he wanted to know from the Italian and made notes in a small pocket-book, scarcely looking up to give a few terse orders when a team of plain-clothes men arrived from Headquarters to examine the room. Without giving any hint that Nadia Tarrant had been murdered the Inspector tested the Italian's alibi, and it seemed valid enough. Then Rodgers told the youth of Nadia Tarrant's death and watched to see how he reacted. Luigi was thunderstruck and in a few seconds he was crying. The Inspector chain-lit another cigarette from the one Mike had offered him and gave the youth several minutes to gain control of himself.

Eventually Saltoni said in a low, shaky voice, 'I always was afraid something would happen to Nadia. She was mixed up in some business but she would not tell me about it. I think perhaps someone was blackmailing her.'

Rodgers leaned forward and spoke quietly. 'Did you, now? That's quite a statement of opinion. Were *you* blackmailing her, by any chance?'

The youth looked at him aghast. 'Me? *Momma mia*, my word of honour, no!'

'Did she ever pay you any money for . . . services, shall we say?'

Saltoni moistened his lips and looked blank. 'I . . . I don't know what you mean. It is true, she lent me ten pounds recently, when I got into debt. That's what I came here for, to pay her back.'

Mike noticed that the Inspector did not let the opportunity slip past. He bent swiftly forward and stretched out his hand. 'Let me see your wallet.'

Saltoni passed the test. There were thirteen pounds in his wallet, ten of them in one pocket. Rodgers nodded and returned the wallet.

Mike said, 'Inspector, do you mind if I ask a question? Luigi, have you heard of a man called Bannister?'

The Italian considered briefly, then shook his head.

The Inspector took over the interrogation once more. 'Suppose you tell me how you first met Nadia Tarrant?'

'It was one of my afternoons off. I remember very well, because it was my birthday. I was lonely and bored, not much money, no friends at that time. I was walking around the streets when I saw a library. I thought, perhaps they have some books in Italian.'

'Which library?'

'It was near Tottenham Court Road. And that is where I met Nadia. She understood some Italian, from the time she was with a circus touring northern Italy. We got talking, and she asked me back here. I liked her, she was kind to me. Later we became . . . very good friends.'

'Quite,' said Rodgers dryly. He considered for a moment, then closed his notebook and stood up. 'Let's leave it at that for the time being. Give your name and address to the Sergeant here and report to my office at nine o'clock tomorrow morning. The Sergeant will tell you how to find it.'

Saltoni gulped in alarm. 'The police station? What for? I have told you all I know.'

'Perhaps. We'll go over it again tomorrow morning. You'll have to sign a written statement. I haven't time to cope with you now.'

Saltoni was plainly upset. The idea of a police station clearly terrified him. 'Inspector, you are making a mistake. I was . . . very fond of Nadia, she was kind to me . . . but we did not see each other very often. Not as often as I wanted. I think perhaps she was trying to avoid me recently.

I was afraid for her – I think she was mixed up in something—'

'Mixed up in what?' Mike cut in sharply. He sensed that the Inspector was frowning impatiently at him, but he felt he must take this opportunity, for it was unlikely that the police would welcome his presence during a second, official interrogation of the youth. Nadia Tarrant, the vital and clearly dubious witness who had done Harold Weldon so much harm, was dead, thus closing a major avenue of investigation; Saltoni represented the only link with her. Mike had to risk incurring the Inspector's displeasure. 'How did you know she was mixed up in something?' he demanded.

Saltoni shrugged his shoulders and knitted his brows in perplexity. 'It is difficult to explain. There were times when she just disappeared, for days on end, a week even. Then when we met again she would not tell me where she had been.'

'Had you ever heard of the Weldon case?'

Saltoni nodded.

'You know that Miss Tarrant was an important witness at the trial?'

'Yes.'

'And you know that Weldon has been condemned to death?'

'It was in the papers.'

'Listen, Luigi, I've got nothing against you. I'm just trying to help Harold Weldon. I think he's an innocent man, and I don't want him to hang for something he didn't do. Did Nadia ever talk to you about Harold Weldon?'

'No. I used to ask her, especially when the trial was on, because I was worried.'

'What about?'

Saltoni looked away evasively.

'What about?' Mike persisted. 'Why were you worried? Go on, tell me.'

Saltoni hesitated, then finally blurted out, 'It is only that . . . the night she said she bumped into Weldon in the Square, she was really with me.'

'Only!' Mike let out a deep breath and exchanged glances with Rodgers, who had sat down again and was breathing heavily. 'Where was she, then?'

Saltoni blurted out the next words like a truant schoolboy at last being forced to tell the truth. 'She came straight to my room from the café and she did not leave until after one o'clock. When I spoke to her about this, afterwards, she told me I was wrong, that it was half-past eleven, but I was not wrong. I remember looking at the clock. It was later, much later.'

Mike turned to the Inspector. 'I understood that Nadia Tarrant – the real Tarrant woman, not the impostor – worked at a restaurant in Greek Street?'

'She did.'

'But either you or John Goldway told me that on the night of the murder she left the restaurant about ten minutes before she bumped into Weldon; somewhere about midnight, in fact.'

Rodgers nodded. 'She did leave the restaurant at about that time. I checked on it during our investigations, naturally.'

Saltoni interrupted, addressing Mike. 'But she did not go straight home. She came to me.'

'She went straight to your room at some address near Euston station? That's nowhere near where she was supposed to have seen Weldon. And you say it was after one in the morning when she left, Saltoni?'

76

'Yes.'

'In other words, she did not bump into Harold Weldon that night, did she? She didn't see him, ever?'

Saltoni squirmed uncomfortably but nodded an affirmative.

Mike turned to the Inspector. 'I certainly think Mr Saltoni should make a written statement for the authorities, Inspector! The sooner the better. This is a lifeline for Weldon.'

'I agree, this is very serious,' Rodgers affirmed. 'I'm not sure that it can wait until—'

He was cut off by the ringing of the telephone, which one of the plainclothes sergeants answered. The man listened briefly and handed the receiver to Rodgers. 'It's for you, sir. I told them where you were to be contacted.'

Rodgers sighed and took the phone. A monosyllabic conversation followed that meant nothing to Mike. He turned away and became aware that Saltoni was trying to attract his attention. The Italian's eyes were flashing some message to him but the youth did not speak; he was obviously scared of the policemen in the room, and it was clear that he wanted to communicate something in private to Mike. Mike nodded imperceptibly and soon afterwards, when Rodgers had rung off, the two men shook hands, and Mike left.

Outside in the Square Mike nodded amiably to the driver of Rodgers's car and strode briskly towards Charing Cross Road. When he judged himself safely out of sight he slipped into a doorway and waited. Several minutes later the police car drove past, the Inspector sitting alone in it.

Mike cautiously made his way back towards Nadia Tarrant's digs. Saltoni was loitering uncertainly at one corner of the Square. Realising that the Italian might still be under observation Mike hailed a passing taxi and ordered the cabbie to drive slowly past where Saltoni was standing. As the taxi drew level Mike told the driver to slow down, at the same time rolling down the window and calling softly to the youth. Saltoni caught sight of him and slipped quickly into the back of the taxi.

'You wanted to see me?' Mike said, as the taxi gained speed.

Saltoni nodded eagerly. 'Yes. I am told that you are not a policeman, Mr Baxter? The Sergeant said you write for the newspapers. Is that the truth?'

'Yes. And if you've got something on your conscience you'd do better to tell it to the proper authorities. Or are you hoping to sell me some information?'

'Sell?' Saltoni looked puzzled and shook his head. 'No, that's not it at all.'

'What do you want, then?'

'I must know . . . what is going to happen to me at the police station tomorrow? What will they do to me? I'm frightened.'

'Just tell the truth, Saltoni, and you've got nothing to be afraid of. They won't beat you up or force illegal confessions from you, if that's what you're thinking.'

'But you forget, I am a foreigner here. You don't know what it is like, having to watch your step all the time. I cannot afford to get mixed up in anything.'

'You're mixed up already, aren't you?' Mike retorted sharply.

'*Momma mia, si!* . . . But . . . Look, Mr Baxter, you think I have behaved very badly over this, don't you? You think I ought to have gone to the police the moment I suspected that Nadia was not telling the truth—'

'And why didn't you?'

'Nadia warned me. She said they would report me to the Ministry of Labour and I would be deported.'

'Rubbish! If you'd told the police the truth they would have been on your side and nothing would have happened to you. Now you'll be asked to make a written statement and there's a big doubt whether they'll believe a word of it.'

'I know. That's what I'm worried about. You must help me.'

'What on earth do you expect me to do?'

'This Inspector, he is a friend of yours, and you have perhaps other important friends. If you say you believe me, that you are willing to . . . what is the word – guarantee? . . . that I am telling the truth, then perhaps I need not . . .' He trailed off into a lame silence.

Mike studied him for a few moments, trying to make up his mind. Eventually he said, 'Saltoni, I think you know a great deal more about this business than you've so far been prepared to admit.'

'I do not! I swear I do not. Please, Mr Baxter, you—'

'What *was* Nadia Tarrant up to? Why did she say she saw Harold Weldon the night Lucy Staines was murdered? Who bribed her?'

'I do not know, honestly I do not know.'

'You must have some idea, some suspicion. She was your mistress, wasn't she? Think back – when was the first time you began to worry about her?'

After a moment's reflection Saltoni answered, 'I wanted to see her one night, but she said she could not manage it. Her sister was ill, she said, and she had to go to Aldershot to see her. I had never heard her mention a sister before. I did not believe her. I thought she was getting friendly with another man. I was jealous and decided to try and follow her. Two times I was not clever enough, but the third time I did not let her out of my sight.'

'And she didn't know she was being followed?'

'No, I was clever. She took the tube train up to Hampstead. She went to a night-club called La Pergola. I felt very ashamed, she did not go to see a man, it was a woman I had seen talking once or twice to Nadia at Farnalio's, where she worked. There was something strange going on between them all the same. Each time when I had come up to where they were talking at Farnalio's they stopped talking when they caught sight of me. I got suspicious.'

'Go on.'

'When I asked Nadia about it she lost her temper, told me to mind my own business.'

'What sort of place was this La Pergola? Perhaps your girlfriend was just asking for a job there.'

'Oh no, it was not at all the kind of place that Nadia could have worked in. It was very smart, very expensive. She was only an unskilled café waitress, you understand. They would not have looked at her.'

'Do you think she had a definite rendezvous with this other woman at La Pergola?'

'I am sure of it. She was obviously waiting for Nadia. I bribed the man at the door, and he told me that they had been there once before together.'

'A pity you couldn't find out the woman's name.'

Saltoni flashed him an excited glance. 'But I did! The doorman told me. Her name is Irene Long, and she works at some smart dress shop in Bond Street.'

Mike sat bolt upright. 'Irene Long, of Conway and Racy's?'

'Yes, that's right.'

'What does she look like? Describe her.'

'She is quite tall, about forty years old, blonde hair but it is not real, I think. She wears a lot of lipstick and stuff.'

'That's her, all right.'

'Do you know her, Mr Baxter?'

'Not as well as I'd like to,' Mike said. 'But that can be remedied.'

Chapter Seven

When Mike got back to the flat Linda greeted him with a quizzical expression.

'I'm so glad you didn't burst in a few minutes earlier. I was having a tête-à-tête with Mr Sanders.'

Mike poured himself the drink he badly needed. 'How very nice for you. What did he want? Does he fancy you as a successor to Irene Long?'

Linda laughed, but her tone became immediately serious. 'No, not exactly. But he seemed to want to find out if I'd seen them both having lunch together.'

'And you said you did?'

'Yes. It didn't throw him for a loop. He muttered the usual thing about being "just good friends".'

Mike pursed his lips. 'It may not be quite as innocent as that, Linda. I've discovered some interesting facts about Miss Irene Long this afternoon and—'

'Let me finish, darling. The real purpose of the Colonel's visit, I'm almost certain, was to find out if I recognized his voice on the telephone at Soho Square. He made up a cock-and-bull story about someone impersonating *his* voice on the telephone at his own flat this afternoon. He says he's

82

been burgled, and the burglar got in by ringing up his house-keeper beforehand and pretending to be Sanders, telling her to put the keys of the flat under the front doormat.'

'Sounds a bit thin,' Mike commented. 'I presume his idea is to persuade us that some brilliant mimic is at large, ringing up left, right and centre – and, amongst other places, Nadia Tarrant's digs. You know, we could always call his bluff by checking up whether his flat really had been burgled.'

'I don't think he'd take very kindly to that.'

'No, I don't suppose he would. There must be subtler ways. Personally, I find this stratagem of his a fairly convincing proof that it *was* he who spoke to you, and that he did recognise your voice and is rather worried about it.'

'I'm sorry, darling, I did try to disguise my voice, but there wasn't much time for rehearsal.'

'Not to worry; sometimes if one throws a spanner in the works all sorts of interesting sparks fly off. Let me tell you what I've found out about the late Nadia Tarrant and her love-life.'

'What about Irene Long?'

'Wait for it – that's the curtain line; the dialogue in between is good too! I just wish Harold Weldon could be here to listen.'

When Mike had finished his account of the hour he had spent with Inspector Rodgers interrogating Saltoni, Linda's eyes were sparkling. 'Darling, this is terrific! It knocks the whole bottom out of the Crown's case against Weldon. Their one and only witness a fraud!'

Mike held up a hand to slow her down. 'Not so fast, old girl! Even if it can be proved that Saltoni is telling the truth and that Nadia Tarrant was indeed sharing his bed at the time she claimed to have seen Weldon – and that's going to be difficult in view of the fact that she is unfortunately dead

– there are still a host of knotty problems to be solved before anyone can ask for a re-trial. I'm inclined to stand by my statement to Weldon this morning: the best way to prove him innocent of the murder is to find out who did do it.'

Linda sighed heavily. 'In other words, a full-scale Baxter investigation, right down the line?'

'Right down to the end of the line, darling. Sorry and all that, but this case has bitten me. I'll crack it if it's the last thing I do.'

'All right, if that's the way you feel, Mike – there's no point in arguing with you. Now what about Irene Long?'

'Saltoni – this boyfriend of Nadia Tarrant's – told me about her, and gave me a good description. It appears there's a very definite connection between the late Nadia Tarrant, who by all accounts was no lily of the field, and our ultra-refined Miss Long.'

'Impossible!'

'That's what I thought. Let me tell you all about it.'

When he had finished describing his strange conversation with Saltoni in the taxi, leaving Linda wide-eyed, he went over to the bookstand housing the bulky volumes of the London telephone directory. In a moment he had found what he wanted and was scribbling down an address. He glanced at his watch. 'Miss Long appears to live out Chelsea way, at 412 Reigate House. Let's get a bite to eat and then corner her in her own den. I don't fancy a private talk with the good lady at her place of work; she can always hide in a changing booth until we go away. We'll go out to her private address, and use your new suit as an excuse. Pretend there's something we're not quite happy about and ask her advice or something. You can always say you didn't have time to get to the shop before closing time.'

'Sounds a bit flimsy – do you think she'll fall for it?'

'She doesn't have to. All I want is my foot in the door.'

A little before eight o'clock the Baxters drove to Chelsea and with the aid of a street map were able to locate the large block of flats where Miss Long lived. The street was narrow and they had difficulty finding a place to park. Mike had just found a spot about one hundred yards from Reigate House when Linda nudged him excitedly.

'Darling, look! Isn't that Mr Staines? Over there, quick! He's just going round the corner.' She pointed to a limping figure.

'Yes, I believe it is!' nodded Mike.

'Does he live this way too?'

'No, he's in Bayswater somewhere, when he's in Town. The Guildford people, Keane Brothers, gave me his private address as well as his City phone number.'

'Do you think he was coming from Reigate House? Has he been visiting Irene Long, I wonder?'

Mike studied the positions of the various buildings and the side street down which Staines had turned. 'Looks rather like it. I don't see where else he could have been, it's a dead end.'

As they watched Staines disappear Linda said, 'I've been meaning to ask you, Mike – were you satisfied with Staines's story about Peggy Bedford and their visit to the Lord Fairfax pub?'

'He certainly wasn't very convincing. What are you driving at?'

'It occurred to me that the Lord Fairfax is about midway between Guildford and Farnham, isn't it?'

'That's correct.'

'And Staines's head office is at Guildford?'

'Right.'

'Where did Inspector Rodgers say Nadia Tarrant's murdered body was found?'

'Farnham. Not bad, dear, not bad at all.'

'You don't sound very impressed. Had you thought it out too?'

Mike smiled and patted her shoulder. 'The thought had actually occurred to me. Don't look so crestfallen, Linda, you're doing very well. I agree, the circumstances appear rather ominous for Hector Staines, who seems to be on visiting terms with Miss Long. And she appears to know a lot of people we would like to know better, such as Sanders, Saltoni and the late Nadia Tarrant.'

He opened the door of the car and slid out. 'Grab your parcel, darling, it's time to get moving.'

Linda picked up the large elegant box in which the suit from Conway and Racy's had arrived that afternoon and together they crossed the road and walked up to Reigate House.

They rang the bell of number 412 and did not have to wait long before the door opened. Miss Long looked momentarily taken aback to see them but she quickly assumed her mask of professional solicitude which she wore all day long at work.

Linda somewhat lamely brought out the lines she had been silently rehearsing during the drive out to Chelsea, ending, 'You see, Miss Long, my husband and I are going abroad almost immediately and time is very short, otherwise I wouldn't have dreamed of troubling you out of business hours.'

'Why, Mrs Baxter, that's quite all right, I'd be only too

glad to help in any way I can. I'm frightfully sorry to hear that the suit isn't quite right, but as you see, I'm just dressing for a dinner date and I'm terribly late as it is. Any other time I'd have been delighted. I promise to be at your sole disposal the very first thing at the shop tomorrow morning.'

Linda was at a loss. 'Yes, that's very kind of you. I quite understand . . . I . . . er . . . So sorry to have been . . .' she faltered, wishing Mike would come to her rescue.

Miss Long favoured him with her scintillating smile. 'I quite understand your wife's concern, Mr Baxter. We women are dreadful fussers over the tiniest thing, you know. If a frock is as much as a quarter of an inch wrong we just don't feel comfortable in it. But I must fly. You *will* forgive me for not asking you in, won't you?'

She was just on the point of closing the door when Mike said smoothly, 'I was hoping to take this opportunity of talking privately to you, Miss Long. About Nadia Tarrant.'

A flicker of alarm appeared in Miss Long's eyes, then her expression went blank. 'Who did you say?'

'Nadia Tarrant. The woman who identified Harold Weldon in the Lucy Staines murder case. You remember it, I dare say,' he added dryly.

'Naturally, Mr Baxter. But I can't imagine why you should want to talk to me about that woman.'

'Wasn't she a friend of yours?'

'A friend? Good gracious me, no!'

'Then let's say acquaintance. Possibly a business acquaintance?'

'I'm afraid you've been misinformed, Mr Baxter,' she replied frigidly. 'I've never met the woman in my life.'

There was a growing note of confidence in her tone which was completely belied by her initial reaction. Mike debated swiftly whether to press the issue. There did not seem much point as long as she continued to keep them on the threshold. 'A pity,' he said. 'I was hoping you might be able to help me in my inquiries.'

'I am sorry,' came the stiff reply.

As they turned to go Linda turned casually and said, 'Oh, Miss Long, my husband and I have been having a little bet just now. He swears he saw Mr Staines leave here just a few minutes ago, and I'm certain he was having hallucinations. Which of us was right?'

'Mr Staines?' she replied, her voice sharp and uneasy. 'You mean Lucy's father?'

'Yes.'

'He certainly has not called here. I've only just got in, and no one called until you rang.'

'There you are, darling,' Linda chortled. 'I keep telling you to see your optician.'

'I'll do that,' said Mike, playing up to her tone. 'Funny – I could have sworn I saw him.'

Miss Long, now completely recovered, smiled evasively. 'I'm beginning to think you imagine things, Mr Baxter. Now I must dash! First thing tomorrow morning, Mrs Baxter, I'll be at your beck and call. Good night.'

As they walked back to the car Linda murmured angrily, 'That's the last time I'll try anything like that, Mike. She made me feel like an unwelcome rent collector.'

'You're too sensitive, darling. You must develop a thicker skin. But she wasn't exactly overjoyed to see us, was she? And what a thundering bad liar she is!'

'I'm not so sure she was lying.'

'About her knowing Nadia Tarrant?' said Mike in surprise.

'Oh yes, she was lying there all right. She couldn't have

been more shocked if you'd hit her on the head with a hat box. But I really felt she may have been telling the truth about not having seen Staines.'

'I'm with you there. She looked scared at the idea, though. Maybe she doesn't want him prowling around the neighbourhood, for some reason or other.'

They reached the car and got in. Mike said, as he started up the engine, 'You're quite sure it *was* Staines that we saw?'

'Yes. Aren't you?'

'Pretty certain. Chalk up one more mystery to be solved. The triangle now has four sides.'

'Geometrically impossible.'

'We started out this evening with a neat triangle of Victor Sanders, Irene Long and Nadia Tarrant. A fairly strong – if for the moment meaningless – line connected all three of them. Now we get Staines apparently trying to force his way into the design. I don't get it.'

'I don't see any design at all, if you draw another line connecting Staines with his late girlfriend, Peggy Bedford.'

'Darling, you are spreading alarm and depression, and my morale is already low enough. Maybe Rodgers will get a break when they question Saltoni tomorrow down at the station. I'm pinning my hopes on that. I've a hunch Saltoni hasn't told all yet.'

It appeared that someone else must have had the same hunch. Scarcely had the Baxters reached their flat than the telephone rang. Linda picked up the receiver, turned pale, and frantically called for Mike, who was in the next room mixing drinks.

'Darling, come quickly! It's a terrible voice – "Mr Baxter, help me!" . . . and then a ghastly groan.'

Mike ran into the room and snatched the receiver.

'Hello? Mike Baxter here . . . Who is it? . . . Luigi? What's happened? . . . Speak up, I can't hear you . . . What's that? Beaten up? . . . Where are you? Where are you phoning from?. . . Louder, man, I can't hear . . . Did you say Euston? . . . The station? . . . Yes, but which tele—' He swore and hung up. 'I think he must have fainted. It's Saltoni, poor devil.'

'You think he's been beaten up?'

'Yes, it sounded like it. He's in a phone booth somewhere on Euston station – heavens, there must be scores of them! Linda, listen! You'd better stay here. Get on to Rodgers and tell him what's happened. If this chap pegs out we haven't a hope of saving Weldon.'

As he hurried out of the room Linda called out frantically, 'Darling, be careful, please!'

The only answer was a slammed door and a few moments later the roar of the Jaguar's powerful cylinders.

Linda telephoned the Yard and asked for Inspector Rodgers. After some delay she was connected. She told the Inspector what had happened.

Rodgers swore briefly. 'Right!' he snapped. 'I'll get on to it immediately! Thank you for calling, Mrs Baxter. I'll look after the ambulance.'

Linda rang off and looked at her watch. It was close on ten o'clock. She asked Mrs Potter to fix some scrambled eggs, and when they came she toyed with her plate as she nervously awaited word from Mike. Eventually, after what seemed an age, the phone rang, but the line was so bad she had difficulty in understanding him.

'Linda? Mike here. Something new has come up. I want you to change your dress – put on that black thing – get a taxi, and meet me by the booking-office on Euston station. Hurry!'

'Can't you come and pick me up, darling?'

'No, I'm all tied up here. Grab a taxi.'

'All right, but why the change of clothes? Are we going somewhere?'

'Yes. I'll tell you all about it when you get here. Do hurry, darling!'

'Right. How's Saltoni?'

'What did you say?'

'I said how's the Italian waiter?'

'Pretty bad. I can't talk now. See you.'

Chapter Eight

Mike spotted her taxi, opened the door, and paid the driver. They walked towards the place where the Jaguar was parked.

'Tell me about Saltoni,' Linda said. 'Is he badly beaten up?'

'Yes. And he doesn't know who did it. He thinks there were two or three of them – they cornered him in a dark alley near his lodgings. I couldn't get much out of him before he fainted again. He was still unconscious when the police arrived, but he did manage to say something about La Pergola night-club. And he said, quite distinctly, "Bannister is the man you want."'

'Bannister! That's the man Sanders referred to when he thought he was talking to the Tarrant woman. Mike, this is exciting – I believe we might be on to something tangible at last! Have you told Inspector Rodgers?'

'There really wasn't much time. I decided not to bother him because he was livid at what had happened and kept blaming himself for not having booked Saltoni on the spot this afternoon. He went off to St Matthew's Hospital with poor old Saltoni – I bet he'll sit like a broody hen at the boy's bedside all night. I did have time whilst waiting for you to give John a ring, though. He seemed to sit up when I mentioned La Pergola, though the name Bannister didn't seem to convey anything.'

'Did he give any indication why La Pergola interested him?'

'Yes. It seems they've had the club under observation for some time. John wants us to meet up with one of his staff; it's a girl called Jo Peters whom he's planted there as a club member. We're meeting her at the top of Baker Street, near the Park entrance, and then going to La Pergola as her guests.'

'Is this Jo Peters very glamorous?'

'Darling, she's a policewoman, I assume. About six feet tall, with flat feet, and shoulders like a sandwich-board, I shouldn't wonder.'

Mike Baxter's guess proved to be a trifle inaccurate. The girl who came swiftly out of the shadows and slipped into their car at the bottom of Regent's Park looked more like a fashion model than a flat-footed policewoman. They wasted little time and sped on their way towards Hampstead.

When the girl spoke her voice was a soft North American drawl, slightly husky and very distinctive. 'We've got about ten minutes for me to put you both in the picture,' she began animatedly. 'My name's Jo Peters and we're supposed to be old friends, so you're Mike and Linda to me, and you call me Jo.' She smiled at Linda and went on, 'It has to be that way, Linda. The Superintendent filled me in on the Weldon case, so I know what you're looking for. I pass as a good-time girl with plenty of money to throw around, given me by my over-fond Daddy. La Pergola isn't cheap so they had to fit me up with a plushy cover. The last time I did a job for Goldway in London was in the Docks, peddling fruit from a barrow, so all this phony glamour makes a nice change.'

'Are you Canadian, Miss . . . er . . . Jo?' Mike asked.

She nodded. 'Now, about La Pergola. We've been watching it for a couple of months or so, not so much the joint itself as the types who go there. The club's clean, but we're not so sure about the clientele.'

'Have you run across a man called Bannister there?'

She shook her head. 'Heard the name for the first time this evening when Goldway was briefing me. He's the one you're looking for, isn't he?'

'Yes. Who runs the club, or owns it?'

'Guy called Charles Corina. He's worth watching. He's some kind of a phony Prince with a Central European background that doesn't quite jell. We're working on it. Vital statistics: dreamy eyes, dark, thirty-sevenish, smooth dancer, slight foreign accent, smooth operator all round, especially with the gals – so watch it, Linda!'

Linda laughed. 'I'm glad there's something in this for me too.'

Jo caught the implication and answered it with typical candour. 'Don't let these war-feathers fool you,' she said, flipping the pearl necklace at her white throat disdainfully. 'It's all borrowed finery and just part of the act. If you want to see the real me just come out to Saskatchewan one summer and watch me handle my Dad's combine harvester.'

'You certainly get around,' Linda remarked enviously.

'What's the main attraction at La Pergola?' Mike asked.

'Charles Corina himself. Oh, the food's good and the floor show is tolerable, but it's Charles they all go to see. The women fight for a place in line so they can dance with him. If he didn't remind me so much of a well-trained snake I'd go for him myself. Give him his due, he works hard keeping everyone happy. Round about two in the morning, though, he disappears. Doesn't say he's going, doesn't say goodnight, just vanishes off the map. Ten minutes later the joint's as dead as an empty barn.'

'He sounds a remarkable young man. How does he manage to keep out of the divorce courts? Sounds like the perfect corespondent,' Linda commented.

Jo laughed. 'Charles is much too clever. I tell you, his technique is worth watching. Well, we're nearly there. I'll have to sign you in, as I'm the only club member here. What name do you want me to put?'

'I think we'd better play it safe – we might be recognised. Just plain Mr and Mrs Mike Baxter,' he decided.

A moment later they pulled into a side street and halted beside a neat pink-and-blue neon sign advertising LA PERGOLA.

Inside the lighting was dim pink and the upholstery was done in a soft pastel blue. A sinuous brunette with a startling *décolletée* was trailing a hand microphone on a small stage, murmuring throaty declarations of love and anguish to the couples drifting on the pocket-handkerchief dance floor. The music from a Latin-American band was excellent of its type, and the place was packed.

Jo signed them in and took Linda to the ladies' powder room whilst Mike drifted casually over to the bar, from which position, perched on a high stool, he had a good view of the hazy, smoke-laden interior. He ordered a gin and tonic from a flaxen-haired barman who badly needed a haircut, and sat sipping his drink, getting the feel of the place.

Finding he was out of cigarettes he asked for a packet and as he paid for them he said in an off-hand voice to the blond bartender, 'Has Mr Bannister been in this evening?'

'Whom did you say, sir?' the barman replied. He had a crisp, faintly Teutonic accent which Mike placed as Bavarian or Swiss.

'Mr Bannister.'

The man shook his head, genuinely puzzled. 'I do not know anyone by that name, sir.'

'Maybe you're new here?'

'No, sir. I am with Mr Corina ever since he has the club.'

It had been worth a try. Mike was fairly certain the barman was telling the truth.

He turned on the stool to look for Linda and Jo, and found himself staring straight into the eyes of Victor Sanders. There was no mirror behind the bar so he had not been aware that anyone had approached immediately behind him.

They exchanged greetings and shook hands rather stiffly. Sanders looked impressive in well-cut evening dress. It suited his ramrod figure and military bearing.

'I didn't know you were a member here, Baxter,' he barked.

'I'm not. A Canadian friend of ours dragged us along.'

'Dragged? You don't sound as if you were enjoying yourself.'

'I might, if I were dressed for the part. You make me feel rather shabby.'

'I shouldn't worry about that. Look around you, there are plenty of others here in mufti. Ah, here's Irene. Let me introduce you.'

As Sanders had been speaking Mike had observed out of the corner of one eye the slow approach of Irene Long towards the bar.

Mike held out his hand. Hers was icy. 'We've already met once this evening,' said Mike, for Sanders's benefit.

Irene Long was embarrassed. 'Yes, Victor. I forgot to tell

you, Mrs Baxter called at my flat just as I was getting ready. She wanted to see me about an alteration to her new suit.'

Sanders frowned heavily, as though not entirely satisfied with a delinquent private's excuse. 'Rather an odd time to call, wasn't it? After business hours?'

Mike came to her rescue. 'My wife and I are off to the South of France very soon, and Linda wants to take the new glad-rags with her, understandably enough. I gather there are three millimetres of lace too much, or something equally world-shattering.'

With a nervous smile Irene Long excused herself and went towards the powder room. Mike and Sanders chatted for a while, then Sanders went off to speak to an acquaintance.

A little while later, as Mike sat at a reserved table with Jo and Linda, he casually remarked, 'There have been some interesting developments whilst you two girls were putting your new faces on. Victor Sanders and his lady are here.'

'I know,' Linda answered. 'I saw you talking to him at the bar and we bumped into Irene Long in the powder room.'

'Any tabs on them, Jo?' Mike asked.

Jo shook her head. 'They're regulars. I've seen them around quite a lot. The woman looked a bit flustered, we thought.'

'What did you do to her, darling? Finally hit her on the head with a hat-box?'

'Simpler than that. She hadn't told the boyfriend about our visit tonight. He didn't seem to like it at all.'

'Interesting. What else had he got to say for himself?'

'He gave me much the same routine as he told you this afternoon, about his flat being burgled by the voice imper-sonator. None of his expensive photographic equipment has been pinched, so he assumes it was Weldon's part of the flat they were searching. I still think he's making it all up. But you should have seen his face when I told him Nadia Tarrant had been murdered. Shook him rigid! And he didn't like the idea of her digs being ransacked either. Just to complete his misery I told him about the missing shoe down at Farnham. I should say I've put paid to his evening fairly comprehensively.'

'Hold everything!' Jo interposed swiftly. 'Here comes the Prince of Glamour himself!'

Mike had somehow expected Charles Corina to look like one of the willowy gigolos of an earlier era, the type seen tripping into *thé dansants* on the Riviera in the wake of corpulent, sex-hungry dowagers. Corina, however, was sunburnt, muscular, with an undeniably aristocratic manner. His movements and figure were those of a man who spends a great deal of the daylight hours keeping in excellent physical condition. Had Mike met him in the street he might have placed him as the owner of a fashionable riding stables. He had a slight foreign accent which did nothing to detract from a considerable stock of charm.

'Jo darling! You look ravishing tonight! Introduce me to your friends.'

'Hi, Charles! I was just going to.'

'Good evening, Mrs Baxter,' he cut in, bowing low and raising Linda's hand to his lips. 'What a pleasure to welcome you here. Good evening, Mr Baxter, we are indeed honoured.'

Mike shook hands stiffly. It was obvious that Corina had been making some discreet inquiries.

Corina bowed to Jo, extended his arm, and swept her off towards the dance floor. The Baxters watched with grudging admiration.

Mike muttered, 'I know it's very British not to be able to

dance decently, but I sometimes wish I didn't feel like such a bull in a china shop when I look at a chap like Corina.'

Linda covered his hand with hers. 'Actually, darling, you do rather well. And some of us girls are allergic to well-trained snakes, as Jo said.'

Mike signalled to a pink-jacketed wine waiter and ordered drinks. 'Just keep your allergies under cover if he asks you for a dance. Pretend you're already drooling over him, but watch your step, he's nobody's fool. Don't try to find out anything about Bannister until the evening's worn on a bit.'

Linda followed instructions and it was not until she had been on the floor with Corina several times that she ventured to bring the topic up. Later she reported back to Mike and Jo.

'I'm afraid I've drawn a blank. He says he'll get his secretary to check the membership list, but my guess is he's got all the names tabulated in that brain of his. And I really don't think he was stalling me, either.'

Mike nodded, not unduly ruffled. 'Never mind, there'll be other sources to try. Were you able to bring the subject round to the Weldon case?'

'Yes. I arrived by devious routes – the coincidence of meeting Irene Long here, my new suit, her job at Conway and Racy's, and so to Peggy Bedford and Lucy Staines.'

Mike poured out more wine. 'Any leads?'

'None at all. I tried him on Nadia Tarrant, too, just to get his reactions; told him she'd been seen at the club. He was highly incensed – said he wouldn't dream of allowing a woman like that in his well-conducted club. When I told him she was seen here with Irene Long he just buttoned up.'

Mike said ruefully, 'We were probably hoping for too

much in expecting the mysterious Mr Bannister to come right out and turn the spotlight on himself.'

Linda turned to Jo. 'The first time you came here, can you remember whom you were with?'

Jo considered for a few moments. 'Yes. Why?'

'I hope his name was Toby Deacon,' said Linda.

Jo shook her head. 'No, I wasn't with any one man. There was a bunch of us, so that I could get submerged in a crowd. There was no Toby Deacon with us, never has been.'

'Damnation!' Linda muttered, toying with her wineglass and looking worried. 'I fell for it!'

'Fell for what?' Jo asked swiftly.

'Corina was trying to catch me out – has done, in fact. He spoke of this Deacon character as if he would be a close mutual friend of ours, and I fell for it. Pretended I knew him too. How could I be so careless? Mike warned me there are no flies on this particular gentleman.'

Their attention was distracted by the resumption of the floor show. When it had ended Mike danced several times with Linda and with Jo.

'I haven't seen any sign of the Colonel and his girlfriend for quite some time,' Mike remarked to Jo. 'I must have upset their evening.'

Jo glanced at her watch as they circled the floor. 'It's nearly two o'clock. Mark my words, Corina will be off in a minute.'

When they returned to their table Linda was looking perturbed. She handed Mike a card with the comment, 'A waiter brought this whilst you were dancing. You aren't going to like it, Jo.'

The message on the card was written in a distinctly foreign handwriting, but the contents were clear enough.

Dear Mr Baxter,

I would like to talk to you privately. My address is 27b South Audley Street. I suggest you call tomorrow afternoon, any time between 4 and 5 o'clock.

Yours sincerely,
Charles Corina

PS. Don't bring your charming friend from Scotland Yard.

Chapter Nine

They made a somewhat silent and depressed trio as they drove back to the West End.

'No ball, no strike, no score,' said Linda ruefully.

'I'm not so sure,' Mike began.

'It's bad that Charles has blown my cover, I admit,' Jo interrupted, 'and Goldway will be furious. I wonder where the leak is? There aren't many people who could have tipped off Corina. But I find it a bit odd, don't you, Mike, that Corina has come out in the open and *admits* he knows I'm working for the Yard? And that he's willing and anxious to do some talking.'

'I'm with you there, Jo,' Mike agreed. 'On the surface we don't appear to have achieved very much this evening, but all the same I'm not quite sure that we haven't stirred up some kind of hornets' nest. It will be interesting to see who gets stung. Now then, where do we drop you, Jo?'

'This corner will do; my place is only a couple of blocks along. Please don't bother to come to the door.'

'Are you sure?'

'I'll get a breath of air before I go in. Thanks for the ride.'

It was nice meeting the two of you – I mean that.'

'It was nice meeting you too, Jo,' Linda said, with genuine warmth. 'Take care of yourself.'

'The correct phrase is, I believe, "Don't take any wooden nickels",' said Mike with a laugh. 'So long, Jo. We'll keep in touch.'

'I think she's rather brave to do that sort of job, and all alone,' said Linda as he restarted the car.

'I expect she can take care of herself. They breed 'em tough out on the prairie.'

As they slowed down for the lights at Marble Arch a taxi drew alongside and Linda suddenly sat bolt upright, stared swiftly for a second, then dropped below her husband's broad shoulder.

'This is my night for seeing things,' she whispered tensely. 'Can you catch a quick look at that woman in the back of the taxi alongside us?'

'Why, who do you think it is?'

'Don't make it too obvious, she might recognise us. Darling, I'll swear it's Nadia Tarrant's double, that tough cookie from Soho Square this afternoon – look out, the lights are changing! Hey, where are you going to?'

For answer Mike swung right along Bayswater in the wake of the taxi. It was of a modern design with a fair-sized rear window and the silhouette of its sole passenger was remarkably reminiscent of the hard-boiled redhead who had duped them and then ransacked the room.

'I could be wrong. I only got a brief look at her,' said Linda excitedly, 'but I could almost swear it *was* her.'

They followed the taxi for several minutes, till Linda exclaimed, 'He's pulling off to the right!'

'See if you can spot what street this is.'

'Too dark. Here's another one – Bolton Gardens – he's turning again. This is Darlington Street.'

'That's strange, I'm sure that name's familiar,' Mike began. 'Hello, he's pulling up.'

He jammed on the brakes and stopped the car some thirty yards behind the taxi. A large head of flaming red hair was visible in the light of the street lamp as the woman got out and paid off the driver. The taxi drove off.

'*It is!* It's her all right!' Linda whispered. 'Look, she's crossing over to the other side.'

'Want to know something interesting?' Mike said in a low voice. 'Hector Staines lives in this street somewhere, I'm almost certain. Darlington Street, I'm sure it was. And the telephone number had a Bayswater exchange too.'

The woman they were watching took a key from her bag and opened the front door.

'Got the house?'

'Yes, the one with the high gables.'

'Right. Let's walk casually past and check the number. There's a phone-box a bit farther up. We'll pop in there and see if it is the same address as Staines's.'

Quietly they left the car and walked up the road, not stopping outside the house with the high gables. 'Two-nine-two,' Mike said softly as they passed, and Linda nodded.

They reached the phone-booth, went inside, and searched rapidly through the S-Z directory for Hector Staines's address.

'Stafford – Stagg – Stainer – Staines . . . Here we are . . . By heavens, I was right! Hector Staines, 292 Darlington Street, W.2,' he said, Linda peering over his shoulder as he found the page. 'This is going to take some explaining, if he really is acquainted with that hard-bitten—'

The rest of his sentence was drowned by the staccato stutter of gunfire, a splintering of glass and the roar of a car engine revving violently. A split second later Mike yelled, 'Down!' as a car swept past the phone-box and reeled with screeching tyres into a vicious left turn.

Mike pulled Linda down and several seconds passed before they stood up again and realised that they had not actually been shot at. The glass of the phone-box was undamaged, and apart from bumps and bruises – as Linda laughingly commented afterwards, it is a physical impossibility for two grown people to duck inside a phone-booth – they were shaken but completely unharmed.

Rather unsteadily they walked to the car and then suddenly stopped short. Every window of the car was splintered with bullet-holes. Anyone sitting inside could hardly have escaped without serious injury.

Mrs Potter announced, 'Superintendent Goldway on the line for you, Mr Baxter.'

'Thank you. Good morning, John.'

'Why ever didn't you ring me last night?' demanded the Superintendent without preamble.

'It was getting on for three in the morning. I hardly liked to disturb you at such an ungodly hour.'

'Another time don't hesitate. Are you both all right?'

'Fine and dandy! Just shaken up a bit, but that's good for the liver.'

'Shaken up sounds an understatement. I've had a look at your Jaguar. She *is* a mess, isn't she? Thank God you weren't sitting in it.'

'And so say all of us!' Mike echoed fervently.

'We're checking on the calibre of bullets now. I'll let you

know what turns up. I imagine you didn't get much of a look at the gunmen?'

'No, not at that speed. It was all over before we knew what was happening. There was also a somewhat embarrassing contest between Linda and myself to see who could hit the deck first.'

'Quite so,' Goldway chuckled, but when he continued his voice was serious. 'Mike, I've got the Sergeant's report on my desk and there are one or two points that puzzle me. I'm tied up this morning but I was wondering if you'll be at home around three o'clock this afternoon?'

'Certainly, if you wish, John. But why don't I come down to the Yard?'

'No, I want to talk to you both, and anyway I've got another call to pay in Belgravia, so it's not out of my way. How did you get on at La Pergola?'

'We drew a blank. But we met some interesting people. I've got a thin line to follow up.'

'Good. How did you like the escort I provided you with?'

'No complaints, Superintendent! No complaints at all.'

Goldway laughed. 'Has she been in touch with you today, by the way?'

'No.'

'Oh. All right. Let me know if she does. I'll be with you soon after three.'

Mike replaced the receiver and grinned ruefully at Linda. 'Cunning old bird, he doesn't miss a trick.'

'He spotted the loophole in our story?'

'He did. It'll be his first question this afternoon.'

It was. Goldway accepted Linda's offer of tea and demanded at once, 'What exactly were you two up to, loitering around

Bayswater at two-thirty in the morning? It's hardly on your route home from Hampstead to Sloane Street. And please don't give me that flimsy line about telephoning for a break-down van because the Jag had packed in. Good enough for the Sergeant but not for me.'

'We *were* in a phone-booth,' Mike temporised. 'Happily for us.'

'Quite so. Now please tell me what you were doing in Darlington Street.'

'We trailed, or think we trailed, a certain lady of dubious character to Hector Staines's home there.'

'The significance of the address had not escaped me,' Goldway observed in a dry tone. 'Who was the lady?'

'I don't know her name, but she has a certain talent for impersonations. She's the one who passed herself off as Nadia Tarrant at that bed-sitter in Soho Square.'

Goldway stiffened. 'Indeed? Where did you stumble across her?'

Mike explained, as Goldway sipped his tea.

'I see,' said Goldway when Mike had finished. 'And you didn't think all this should have appeared in the police report you gave to the Sergeant?'

Mike hesitated, and when he finally spoke he chose his words with care, causing the Superintendent to look up. 'No, John, I did not think everything need appear in that report.'

'Very well, Mike. No doubt you have your reasons.'

There was a delicate pause, but Mike was too unsure of the theory that was gradually forming at the back of his mind, and Goldway knew him and trusted him too well to press the issue. He changed the conversation abruptly.

'Mike, I'm none too happy about Jo Peters. She hasn't checked in, and we haven't been able to contact her all day.

Do you think she might have phoned you whilst you were out?'

Mike glanced at Linda and shook his head. 'No, we've been in most of the day, except for a useless visit to Conway and Racy's. Anyway, Mrs Potter would have taken a message.'

'Quite. It's rather worrying. She was supposed to call me this morning and report on your combined operations of last night. When she didn't I told my secretary to contact her. There was no answer. Finally I put a man on the job and it appears she never even went back to her flat last night.'

'But we took her home ourselves!' Linda protested.

'Right to the door?'

'Well, no, not exactly. But she said it was only a few yards away.'

The Superintendent frowned thoughtfully. 'There's probably nothing to worry about, she's a very capable girl. However, the night porter at the block of flats where she lives is quite positive she didn't return there – he's on duty till seven in the morning. And the bed's definitely not been slept in.'

Linda put in, 'How long has Jo been working for you, John?'

'About three years, on and off. Her position's rather a peculiar one – although she's attached to the Yard she's not on what we call the established staff.'

'Does she work for Inspector Rodgers?'

'No. She doesn't work for any of the regular CID people,' said Goldway vaguely, and it occurred to Mike that he was evading the question. 'She's answerable to her own . . . department, and to me personally.'

'What exactly was she doing at La Pergola?'

Goldway hesitated. 'Let us say, keeping an eye on the place.'

There came a knock at the door and Mrs Potter entered.

'Excuse me for intruding, Mrs Baxter, but there's a parcel addressed to you. Found it outside the door. It wasn't there a couple of minutes ago when I put the milk bottles out.'

Mrs Potter handed Linda a neatly wrapped box. She examined the address, which was printed in large capital letters. It told her nothing.

'You've no idea who delivered it, Mrs Potter?' she said.

'No, ma'am. Whoever it was, he didn't ring the bell.'

Linda frowned. 'Probably something we ordered,' she decided, and was just about to cut the string with her nail scissors when Goldway put out a restraining hand.

'Wait a moment, Linda,' he cautioned. 'These things have been known to explode. I'd better take it along to the Yard and let them examine it.'

'But, surely,' Linda was beginning to protest when Mike snatched up the parcel, held it in both hands for a moment as if appraising it, then snapped the string.

'Mike, don't be a fool,' Goldway protested, trying to restrain him.

'It's all right, John. I've a pretty shrewd idea what's inside.'

He took off the wrapping to reveal an ordinary cardboard box. Then he lifted the lid and looked at the object inside for a few moments.

'Just as I thought,' he said. 'Another woman's shoe.'

Goldway asked uneasily, 'One of yours, Linda?'

Linda shook her head. 'No, I wish it were. Recognise it, Mike?'

'I'm afraid so. Jo Peters was wearing exactly that style last night.'

There was a long silence.

Eventually Linda said, in a voice that faltered, 'Does it mean what I think it means, John?'

'It's bad, that's clear enough. Just how bad, it's hard to guess.'

Mike broke in with unwonted sharpness. 'When Lucy Staines was murdered a shoe was stolen. When Peggy Bedford committed suicide a shoe was missing. And Nadia Tarrant had one shoe missing when they found her strangled in the Farnham woods. Death and a missing shoe, each time. I don't see much scope for guessing.'

'There's just this subtle difference, Mike,' Goldway pointed out patiently. 'In the three instances you mention the shoe was missing, and despite all our efforts none of them has been found. But this time we actually *have* the shoe. It's not missing, it's here, right in front of our eyes. I have a strong conviction that this time there is no death associated with it – I hope to God I'm right! This shoe has been sent as a symbol, to warn us; to warn you, most of all, and Linda.'

Mike grunted. 'I certainly look forward to my talk with Corina,' he said, glancing at his watch.

Goldway shot him a questioning look and for answer Mike produced the note Corina had had delivered to him in the night-club. When Goldway came to the final line his face went dark with anger. 'So Corina's tumbled to Jo! I'd give my pension to know how that leaked out.'

'Perhaps you'd tell us now just why Jo was watching La Pergola?' Mike ventured.

Goldway gave him a level look, then appeared to make up his mind to the inevitable. He considered for a moment, then nodded. 'You know I trust you, Mike, but caution is inbred deep in all of us in this game. However, there doesn't seem to be much point in trying to protect Jo now that the cat's out of the bag. Jo was seconded to us from the Federal Bureau of Narcotics, Washington. That's the "department" I was referring to. She was following a trail of drugs that stretched across the Atlantic and appeared to lead to Corina. We never got anything definite and now it looks as if we never will.'

'Drugs? I wondered about that,' said Mike. 'Tell me, John, how large and valuable a quantity of the stuff could be hidden in, say, the heel of a lady's shoe?'

'I see what you're getting at, Mike. Yes, it's certainly a possibility.'

There was another silence whilst the Baxters digested this new twist to the Weldon case.

Eventually Linda said, 'Do you suppose Luigi Saltoni was mixed up in this dope smuggling too?'

'It's possible.'

'What's his physical condition today?'

'Still pretty much under the weather.'

'Have you any objection to my seeing him?' Mike asked.

'No, of course not.'

'I'm glad to hear it. I telephoned the hospital this morning and they said he wasn't allowed to take any messages or receive any visitors.'

'That's just a precautionary measure. We dare not risk anything happening to him. The rule doesn't apply to you, Mike.'

Further discussion was interrupted once again by Mrs Potter, who tapped on the door and came in to announce Hector Staines.

'I wonder what the dickens he wants?' Mike said irritably. 'Put him in the study, Mrs Potter. I don't know what he's after, but I'm certainly going to take this opportunity of asking him a few blunt questions.'

'Such as?' Goldway asked.

'Such as why he called on Irene Long last night – if he did, that is. We're pretty sure we saw him in the vicinity. Secondly, why he took Peggy Bedford to a remote country pub near Farnham. Thirdly, what his relationship is to the red-headed menace who passed herself off as Nadia Tarrant.'

'I've no doubt this will amuse you,' said Linda, 'but my feminine intuition tells me Staines is in the clear. We can't overlook the fact that he was the first person to draw our attention to the Weldon case. Let me try and answer those three questions of yours for him, darling. "I, Hector Staines, visited Irene Long because she was a friend of my late daughter and I am trying to discover what I can about who framed Harold Weldon. Question Number Two: I did not take Peggy Bedford to the Lord Fairfax, she took me, and that's why I failed to notice the name of the pub; I was in love with her, or I was having an affair with her, or more simply she too was a friend of Lucy's. Third question: What red-headed menace are you talking about? No one of that description came to see me at Darlington Street last night, so you must have been mistaken, Mr Baxter." There, how's that?'

Mike looked unconvinced, but made no reply.

Goldway replaced his teacup and stood up. 'I must be on my way. I don't particularly want to encounter Staines, but if you think the time is ripe I'll get Rodgers to have him in and try a little hard cross-examination.'

'Not yet, John. I'll let you know, if I may? Before you go, though—' Mike went to a drawer and extracted a photograph. 'Do you recognise this customer?'

Goldway took the snapshot and examined it carefully. 'Yes, it's the late Larry Boardman, alias Leonard Bradley, alias about six other names. Jewel thief, confidence man, trickster. He died a short time ago – of natural causes, strange to say. Where did you find this?'

'Amongst Peggy Bedford's possessions in her flat. I went back there after her suicide and managed to . . . er . . . persuade the porter to open up for me. I was looking for the missing shoe – or any other likely clue. Boardman's picture struck me as being possibly significant.'

'Quite so. It has been established that Miss Bedford had a wide and somewhat dubious circle of acquaintances. She left an address book that has been quite a revelation. 'No,' he added with a dour smile, 'there was no Bannister in it. Some other names from what we like to call the Top Drawer, but that's rather beside the point.' He looked at his watch, 'Heavens, I must be off, I'm late! Phone me the moment you hear anything from Jo, won't you? Thank you for tea, Linda, my dear.'

Mike conducted the Superintendent to the door, and was about to go through into the study where Hector Staines was waiting when Linda intercepted him.

'Not so fast, Mike. I want a word with you first.'

'Really, darling? What about?'

'Don't come the old innocent on me! Why didn't you tell me you'd bribed your way back into Peggy Bedford's flat?'

Mike grinned. 'Perhaps I was hoping to erase my name from that spicy address book of hers.'

'Fiddlesticks! Who was Larry Boardman? Where does he fit into this?'

Mike sighed impatiently. 'I'd explain if I could, but my theory's only just beginning to take shape. I'll tell all once I understand it myself. Be patient, darling, the case may split wide open sooner than we had dared to hope. Corina's the next on the list, once I've got rid of Staines, and then we're going to St Matthew's Hospital for a chat with Luigi Saltoni.'

She tidied up the tea-things and about five minutes later heard Staines leave.

When Mike came in the room again she asked, 'Did you fire those three questions at him?'

'I did.'

'And?'

'You might almost have rehearsed him in the answers. But all the same,' Mike added vehemently, 'that old bird is hiding something or I'm the village idiot! He even pretends he didn't hear any shooting last night; says he was in his bath!'

'People do have baths at the oddest hours. Maybe he sings in his and so drowned the noise. What did he want to see you for?'

'Everyone in the area was questioned by the police this morning. He seemed to want to clear himself with me, to convince me he had nothing to do with the affair.'

'Perhaps he's telling the truth.'

'He hasn't *started* telling the truth yet!' Mike snapped. 'I tackled him about Bannister, but he just looked blank. He also says he received no visitors last night, so I didn't think it necessary to tell him why we were in the neighbourhood at two-thirty in the morning.'

'So what's the next move?'

'I'm due at Corina's. Are you going to take another crack at Irene Long, darling?'

Linda nodded. 'I thought I would. She can't possibly be having a "coffee break" all day long. Watch your step with the glamour boy, won't you?'

'I will. See you at the hospital around five. And tell Mrs Potter to stick around in case Jo tries to call us.'

Charles Corina's suite of rooms in South Audley Street was an eye-opener. Mike's first impression was that he had strayed into a room in one of Ludwig II's castles in Bavaria. On a beautifully polished parquet floor of intricate design lay a few costly rugs; dim etchings of market squares and Rathaus buildings belonging to long-bombed European cities hung on the cream walls; and a fine collection of delicate china – Mike recognised Delft, Dresden and Spode, amongst others – lined the shelves of a period dresser. Tooled leather books in several languages denoted the man's wide range of interests. But there were also, scattered amongst the *objets d'art*, several statues and small silver trophies of a distinctly equestrian nature, and above the escritoire hung a photograph of Corina in polo kit mounted on a fine white horse. Across the open fireplace hung two fencing foils. The two sides of the man's personality, the intellectual and the physical, were on view for the perceptive observer. The man he had to deal with was no ordinary night-club manager or lounge lizard, Mike reminded himself.

Corina offered drinks, which Mike declined.

'You know why I wanted to see you, of course?' Corina began, raising his brandy glass and drinking his guest's health with a stiff little Continental bow. His accent, Mike noted again, was very slight and an undoubted part of his stock of charm. Mike decided to let his host make the running.

'No, Corina, I haven't the slightest idea.'

'Come, come, my dear fellow – I should have thought it was obvious to a man of your perspicacity.'

'You flatter me.'

Corina smiled. 'You received my note?'

'That's why I'm here.'

'I'm afraid you've made me a little angry by your actions.'

'What actions?'

'Why did you set your watch-dogs on La Pergola? I detest being spied upon.'

'Watch-dogs? You mean Miss Peters?'

'Precisely.'

Mike shrugged his shoulders. 'That was none of my affair, Corina. I only met the girl for the first time last night.'

'I gleaned that from your wife,' Corina answered with a complacent smile.

'And I don't know how you found out Miss Peters's connection with Scotland Yard.'

'She draws her salary there.'

'Are you sure? Even if she does, I doubt if it's a very princely one. Be that as it may, I myself am not and never have been attached to the police.'

'Then why this snooping round my province?'

'I thought I made that quite plain last night, or rather my wife did. I'm looking for a man named Bannister.'

'I assure you there is no such person of that name in—'

'And I would also appreciate a little information on Nadia Tarrant's connection with your club.'

Corina was really annoyed now. 'If you and your friend Superintendent Goldway really imagine I would allow a woman like that inside an *élite* club—'

'Then you do admit to knowing her?'

Corina parried superbly. 'I have not been vouchsafed that dubious pleasure.' Like all foreigners who have taken immense pains to master the English language his vocabulary was studded with words no ordinary Englishman would consider using. 'I am, however, capable of reading English, or what passes for it in the common Press. Nadia Tarrant was the faded music-hall performer in the Weldon case, I seem to recall.'

'Yes, she was. I use the past tense with care. She was found drowned in a river near Farnham yesterday.'

Mike had set the trap with care. The details of the killing had not yet been released. Only the murderer and a handful of police investigators knew that she had been strangled in some woods.

Corina passed the test with ease. 'More fool she. She should have stayed away from the water.'

Mike drew a deep breath. 'I'd still like to know,' he went on, 'what she was doing at your club in the company of Irene Long?'

Corina sighed. 'This is going to be duller than I had thought. Perhaps you did not hear me. I repeat, no circumstances on earth would force me to tolerate a common creature like that in my establishment.'

'All right, have it your way: no Bannister, no Tarrant – but what about a youth named Luigi Saltoni? You know him?'

'No, I don't know him. Who or what is Saltoni?'

'He's also part of the Weldon case,' Mike replied evasively.

'Is that to be your only topic of conversation?'

'For the time being, yes. The Weldon case and La Pergola night-club.'

'I assure you, Mr Baxter, there is no connection.'

'I think there is. Saltoni definitely said he saw Irene Long, whom you'll admit is a club member, entering your very exclusive "establishment" with Nadia Tarrant.'

'Then Saltoni is a liar.'

'That remains to be proven. Look, Corina, if your

conscience is clear then there's no earthly reason why you should obstruct me in my efforts to save an innocent man from hanging – unless it's the bad publicity you're afraid of, when word gets around about dubious characters seen at La Pergola. If that's the case I promise to do what I can to keep La Pergola's name out of it.'

Corina's tone was icy. 'Thank you, but I prefer to handle my own public relations. I'm quite capable of protecting the good name of my club without your heavy-handed assistance.'

'I should weigh those words, if I were you. I offered my help, but if you refuse to co-operate I may go over to the offensive.'

'I doubt if you can do me much harm,' Corina snapped contemptuously.

'No? I have many friends in Fleet Street, Mr Corina.'

Corina turned his back and poured himself another drink. When he faced Mike he was in complete control of himself.

'You know, Baxter, what irritates me about this whole silly rigmarole more than anything else is your continued insinuation that the behaviour and actions of a criminal can be laid at my door.' He waved a hand round the room at his collection of priceless *objets d'art*. 'Is that really how you judge me?'

Mike got up and walked casually to the fireplace. He fingered the fencing foils. 'Skill on the dance floor and a taste for ceramics, Corina, do not rule out a talent for more active pastimes, it would appear. Suppose you quit stalling and tell me just how you learnt that Jo Peters was attached to the Yard?'

'Someone breathed it in my ear. I have a wide circle of

friends. It is one of the pleasures of being in the entertainment business.'

'Did this friend have a name?'

'Even if I could remember I would not be so naïve as to tell you. I did not even believe it at first. In fact, it was not until I received official confirmation from the police themselves—'

Mike was startled. 'The police?'

'Yes. It was a small matter of the loss of a ring by one of our club members. The insurance firm reported it to Scotland Yard and Inspector Rodgers came to make a routine inquiry.'

'And I suppose Inspector Rodgers blandly told you that Scotland Yard had planted Miss Peters in your midst?'

'You don't appear to listen very carefully, Baxter. I said no such thing. Rodgers was far too absorbed in playing his self-appointed role of cautious investigator to do more than look dumb – his usual expression. – when I challenged him over Jo. But officers of the law make poor actors. I obtained the confirmation I needed for what had already been whispered in my ear.'

They eyed one another with undisguised dislike, and Mike reached for his hat, mentally shrugging his shoulders. The smoothness of the man's verbal technique rivalled his snake-like grace on the dance floor. Only at one point during their fencing did Mike feel he had struck home: with his hint of unfavourable publicity for Corina's club. He decided on his Parthian shot.

'I've tried playing it nicely, Corina. I can play it rough too. If you continue to obstruct me I'll break your night-club into twenty different pieces. The only customers you'll have inside La Pergola will be newspapermen and probing police officers. Do I make myself clear? Furthermore, I promise you that if anything happens, or has happened, to Jo Peters you'll find me with a heavy crowbar right in front of that neon sign of yours.'

Corina had visibly recoiled at the intensity of Mike's vehemence. Making a gallant effort to recover the situation he held open the door and bowed slightly as Mike swept past. 'Whatever happens to Miss Peters,' he said, 'is of no possible concern to me. I am simply not interested in the young lady.'

'That's not what I'm getting at, Corina!' Mike ground out savagely. '*She* was interested in you.'

Chapter Ten

'Someone has certainly rubbed you up the wrong way,' said Linda with a half-anxious, half-joking glance at her husband as they walked down the wide flight of steps from St Matthew's Hospital. 'Was Corina very rude or has Saltoni upset you?'

'The answer is "yes" to both questions. Corina made my blood boil but told me nothing of any value. He seemed to think *I'm* responsible for having his club watched.'

'Did you tackle him about Jo's disappearance?'

'Yes. He pretended to be surprised, and then plain indifferent. I didn't believe him. He's a tough customer behind all that suave charm.'

'And Saltoni?' Linda asked, glancing over her shoulder at the hospital they had just left; she had arrived too late to accompany Mike into the Italian's room.

Mike swore expressively. 'The little skunk's clammed up!'

'Oh no! You don't mean he's withdrawing his statement about Nadia Tarrant being in bed with him that night?'

'I do. Now you know why I'm furious. Someone's been at him and scared him into changing his mind.'

'But that's impossible! He's not been allowed any visitors, surely?'

'That's true, so far as it goes. No one but the police and the hospital staff have been allowed into his room.'

'Then how on earth could he have been contacted?'

Linda led the way to their hired car and slipped behind the wheel.

Mike got in beside her and said, 'It can't have been too difficult. A telephone message, a note slipped under a plate of food, or even a bit of skilful bribery of one of the hospital staff – one of the stretcher-bearers, perhaps, or a cleaner. No violence would be needed, just a message threatening him with worse than a beating-up if he failed to retract his statement. I was a fool not to have foreseen the possibility.'

'Bang goes our one and only ally,' said Linda thoughtfully. 'The elusive Mr Bannister, if that's the man behind this murky business, seems always one jump ahead of us, doesn't he?'

'He certainly seems well informed about what's going on.'

Mike lit a cigarette. 'How did you get on with Irene Long, by the way? Or hasn't she finished her morning coffee break yet?'

Linda sighed gloomily. 'She put on the big act about being terribly busy. Short of running round the store like a lost hound I couldn't very well pin her down. I did manage to throw a few names at her, such as Staines and Corina, but apart from turning bright pink when I mentioned Victor Sanders she sidestepped the lot.'

'That fits, anyway,' said Mike enigmatically. He glanced at the dashboard of the car in which they sat. 'Can you drive this thing?'

'Certainly, sir. A trained chauffeuse was part of the hire contract! Is there anywhere you wished to go, sir?'

'Yes, Miss. Tottenham Court Road.'

She was about to release the clutch when she hesitated. 'There's Inspector Rodgers going into the hospital.' She pointed.

Mike swung open his door, stood up, and called across the parking area to the Inspector.

He turned, gave a friendly nod, and came over to the car, greeting them both politely but in a preoccupied manner.

'You've been to see Saltoni?' he asked.

'Yes,' Mike answered. 'I was in there for a few minutes.'

'How is he?'

'He seems to be suffering from temporary amnesia,' was Mike's dry comment. 'Can't remember what he told us yesterday afternoon.'

Rodgers muttered an imprecation. 'You mean he's trying to go back on what he said about the Tarrant woman?'

'Not trying to – he's gone.'

'Blast!' Rodgers muttered. 'How the devil do you suppose this happened?'

Mike shrugged his shoulders. 'I'm afraid it's rather obvious. Someone must have scared him to death – or rather, to silence and loss of memory.'

Rodgers nodded gloomily. 'I've been too tied up to be able to get down before. I haven't seen him since I brought him in, unconscious, late last night. I left strict instructions that no one was to be allowed into his room.'

'Nevertheless, he's been got at. There's always someone who has to bring a patient his food or make his bed. Maybe a ward cleaner, or a nurse; and I noticed there's a telephone in his room.'

'I left orders that no calls were to be accepted. So it can't be that. No letters or messages were to be delivered, either.

123

Someone's bungled. Believe you me, there's going to be a very thorough check here, from the Head Matron and the Chief Surgeon downwards.' He touched his hat and turned to go.

'Is there any news of Jo Peters?' Linda called out.

Rodgers turned. 'No, there isn't, I'm afraid. Goldway mentioned that she hadn't reported to him today. By the way, Baxter, did *you* know she was attached to Scotland Yard – that she was watching La Pergola?'

'As a matter of fact I did, Inspector.'

Rodgers made a grimace of annoyance. 'Well, it was news to me. It's a pity the Superintendent didn't mention her before. It always helps for the right hand to know what the left hand is doing.'

'She wasn't actually working on the Weldon case, you know.'

Rodgers sniffed. 'That makes a nice change, anyway. Just about everyone else seems to be in on it.'

Mike and Linda exchanged an embarrassed look; evidently the news about Saltoni had put Rodgers in a foul mood.

Mike took out his cigarette-case and offered it to the Inspector, saying, 'You mentioned just now that you didn't know Jo was working for the Yard. Didn't Charles Corina mention her to you?'

'Corina? The fellow who runs La Pergola?'

'Yes.'

'No. Why? Surely he didn't know about the Peters girl as well?' Rodgers asked.

'As a matter of fact he did. And he insists that he asked *you* whether she was working for the Yard.'

'Well, well! And what am I supposed to have said in this highly interesting conversation?'

'Apparently you were non-committal,' Mike replied.

Rodgers gave the ghost of a smile. 'I'll bet I was. What an imagination that character's got!'

He turned and strode with large, purposeful steps towards the hospital.

Linda watched his broad back and shivered. 'I'm rather glad I'm not at the receiving end of one of the Inspector's cross-examinations. I feel almost sorry for Saltoni. Rodgers is a pretty tough old brute, isn't he?'

'His line of business tends to bring him into contact with little else than equally tough old brutes. Occupational hazard, the trick-cyclists call it. Now then, miss, if you've got nothing better to do, would you care to drive this expensive wagon towards the library off Tottenham Court Road?'

'Certainly, sir!' Linda grinned and switched on the ignition. 'Being merely the chauffeuse, I don't suppose you'd care to tell me why we're going there?'

'It happens to be the place where Saltoni first met Nadia Tarrant.'

'What's so startling about that?'

'It strikes me as being an odd place for a couple like that to run across one another.'

Linda looked puzzled. 'I don't get it. She was probably changing her latest lurid novelette and—'

'It isn't that sort of library. No novelettes allowed inside the door. Chiefly large, dry, dusty tomes full of facts and no fiction. Nadia Tarrant, from what I can judge of her, was hardly the type of woman to go there unless she had a specific purpose. I want to find out what it was.'

Standing to one side in the library Linda watched with amusement as Mike turned on the charm for the benefit of the elderly, rather frigid female assistant whom he had singled out to help him. In less than a minute he had secured her co-operation.

'Perhaps you'd be so very kind as to tell me the procedure here. I mean does one have to give one's name in order to get a book?'

'Certainly.'

'And the exact procedure . . . ?' Mike pressed, giving her his most winning smile.

'You consult the catalogue, decide which book you want, then write the number of the book together with your name and address on a slip of paper. We take the slip and give you the book. You can't take it away, of course, you have to read it on the premises.'

'I see. And what happens to the slip?'

'We're supposed to file them, but sometimes they get destroyed.'

'Well, you see,' Mike went on, 'a friend of mine – she's fairly tall, about forty, with bright red hair – consulted a book on April 14th and she can't remember the title, but she insists I ought to read it. Do you think it would be possible to look up the slip and . . .'

'Well, I don't know . . . it's a little unusual . . .'

'Yes, I do realise that,' Mike said with a disarming smile, 'but I should be most grateful if you would . . .'

'Very well, I'll have a shot at it,' the librarian said.

'This is really most good of you.'

'Not at all. I expect I'll find it if we've still got it. What's the name of your friend?'

'Miss Tarrant. Miss Nadia Tarrant.'

'All right, sir. If you'll just take a seat . . . I won't be long.'

'Thank you.'

Whilst the elderly assistant went away to rummage amongst several box-files Linda said quietly to Mike, 'Why do you want to know the name of the book?'

'I'm curious, that's all.'

'But why? I can't see that it matters what she was reading. I expect it was a filthy day and she just popped in here to get out of the rain.'

Mike smiled. 'It was a very nice day, as it happened.'

Linda gazed at him in disbelief. 'You're not trying to tell me you remember what the weather was like on every day last April?'

'No. I asked Saltoni. The weather was perfect; he remembers because it was his birthday. That's what started my brain ticking.'

The assistant had returned and was beaming at Mike. He hurried to the desk.

'You're in luck,' she said. 'I've found the slip. On the 14th of April a Miss Nadia Tarrant of Soho Square asked for two books. *The Theory of Photographic Process* – that's a well-known reference book on the subject; and the second one was *Encyclopaedia of the Social Sciences*. Perhaps you've heard of it?'

'The one edited by Sir Ronald Bakerton?'

'That's right. It's quite a recent publication.'

'I see. I wonder if I could have a look at them?'

The assistant looked unhappy. 'I thought you might ask. By bad luck they're both at our Edgware branch at the moment.'

'Never mind, I'm a bit short of time anyway. I'll call another day. You've been most helpful. Thank you so much.'

'Not at all, sir, it was a pleasure.'

'Has all that got you any farther forward, darling?' Linda asked as they drove home.

'I think it has. The significance of a book on photography will hardly have escaped you, surely?'

'You mean Sanders? Perhaps it's pure chance that he happens to be a keen amateur photographer.'

'Perhaps.'

'What about the other book – "Social Sciences" or something?'

'I'll pass an opinion on that when I've had a chance to study it. Home, James, and don't spare the horses!'

'Why don't we call in at a good bookshop on the way home?'

'Both books are likely to be pretty hefty tomes, I doubt if many places would have them in stock. Besides, it's too late now, darling. It's after six. No, we can save time in the morning by phoning around. I'll get them sent up by special delivery.'

Linda and Mike had scarcely arrived back at their flat when the telephone rang. It was Superintendent Goldway.

'Is that you, Mike? I've been trying to reach you for the last half-hour . . . But never mind the apologies, something important's come up. We've picked up Jo.'

'Have you indeed! Where? How is she?'

'Roughed up a bit, I'm afraid. But alive, and she'll shortly be kicking! We found her wandering in a semi-drugged condition near her flat this afternoon. We've got her safely tucked in bed now.'

'Semi-drugged? How do you mean?'

'They shot her full of that damned "truth drug".'

'Does she know who did it?'

'She's fairly certain who's behind it, but there's not a lot to go on at the moment. Can you get down here? I'd like you to hear the full details. Maybe you can talk to her later on when she's slept it off a bit. Oh, and tell Linda to get her glad-rags ready, you're both on the dancing shift again tonight!'

'Same place, John? We're not members there, you know.'

'Don't worry, Mike. That's all arranged.'

Mike was able to give Linda an account of his interview with Goldway as they drove later that evening to La Pergola.

'So there really is a Mr Bannister behind all this? Saltoni wasn't lying?' Linda asked.

'There's a Mr Bannister all right. Only we don't know what he looks like. Some thug threw a sack over Jo's head and bundled her into a car. It must have happened only a few minutes after we dropped her off last night. It was a gang of about three or four, Jo thinks, and the interesting thing is one of them jumped the gun and began asking her questions in the car. The thug driving it yelled at him to shut up, and said, "Bannister will do the questioning". She doesn't think the others noticed the slip-up.'

'Where did they take her to?'

'She doesn't know, but it was quite a way out of town, unless they drove around in circles to confuse her. She has a feeling it was some sort of lonely mansion – there were leaves and gravel beneath her feet and she heard a dog barking across empty space – Jo's been trained to notice things like that. Then she was led into a large room and placed in front of a blinding light. The questions were put to her by a man wearing a nylon mask, but he wasn't the one in charge; there was some figure in the shadowy background who was constantly consulted. He kept his voice low and Jo couldn't hear what he said, but the lilt of his voice and some hint of an accent made her think it might be a foreigner.'

'Corina!'

'Possibly. The line of questioning fits too. They kept hammering away at why she had been sent to watch La Pergola. She tried to play it dumb but they wouldn't swallow that, of course. They tried to find out if she knew who Bannister was, too, and if she was snooping around for some leads in the Weldon case. She denied this flatly, of course, whereupon they grew a trifle annoyed and knocked her around a bit. Those are her own words and it sounds like the under-statement of the year.'

'Poor Jo. It's dreadful. My hunch was right, when I felt worried for her last night.'

'Apparently the rough stuff didn't get them anywhere, so then they pumped this drug into her. It was then she must have spilled the beans about working for the Narcotics Bureau in Washington and Goldway's dope-peddling investigations. The odd thing is she got the impression that none of her later revelations caused much dismay. Their chief concern seemed to be whether she knew who Bannister was. It's just possible they're in the clear as far as drug smuggling is concerned.'

'Do we know for sure why they sent us one of her shoes?'

'Either to try and scare us, or to bluff us into assuming a connection with the Weldon case. Contradictory, I realise, but it could really be either.'

'You haven't actually seen Jo, then?'

'No, she's still pretty woozy, I gather.'

'What does Inspector Rodgers think about all this?'

'I don't know; he wasn't there when I talked with John.

But the old boy will naturally have put him in the picture by now. I expect Rodgers will be at La Pergola tonight.'

'Why don't they simply arrest Corina?'

'No, there isn't enough evidence to make it stick. Jo *thinks* it was Corina conducting the interrogation through this middle-man, but she can't be sure. And don't forget we still have to prove that Corina and Bannister are one and the same person. That's why we're hanging on to La Pergola like a bunch of leeches in the hope of scaring Corina into a false move. He's a slippery customer but if we put the wind up him enough he may give himself away.'

Linda nodded and slowed down as they entered the outskirts of Hampstead. 'And my share of the proceedings is to drop heavy hints about your pals in Fleet Street, is that right?'

'Yes. That's about the only thing I can think of that might get Corina rattled.'

'I'd like to drop something heavier than that on him!'

'So would I. Don't put ideas into my head! Here we are.'

The evening was not a success. After they had been there for nearly an hour with no sign of Corina putting in an appearance Mike grew impatient.

'If Mahommed doesn't come pretty soon to the mountain, then this little mountain is going to do some prowling around backstage.'

Linda shook her head dubiously. 'The place seems much too quiet,' she said.

Mike finished his drink. 'Corina's probably heard we're here and is ducking out of sight in his office.'

'With four or five enormous thugs acting as bodyguards, darling. You'd never get in – or out again, in one piece.'

'We'll see about that,' said Mike, on the point of rising.

'Hold it, darling, there's Inspector Rodgers, just coming in. He gets paid for the rough stuff, leave it to him.'

The Inspector had caught sight of them and was cutting a none-too-polite swathe through the drifting couples on the dance floor.

'He's looking rather pleased with himself, don't you think?' Linda added.

'Let's hope he has good grounds. Hello, Inspector. Enjoying yourself?'

Rodgers scowled contemptuously round the room. 'Nothing but the call of duty would ever bring me to a place like this.'

'La Pergola's chief attraction seems to be having a night off.'

'Corina? He's in his office. I've just seen him.' He winked broadly. 'I have an idea he's not feeling too well this evening. At least, he wasn't when I left him.'

'Did you two have a difference of opinion?'

Rodgers smiled thinly. 'Let's say he caught his foot in the carpet and fell rather clumsily.'

Mike grunted with satisfaction. 'You can't make an omelette without breaking some eggs.'

'He's a very smooth customer, though,' Rodgers went on pensively. 'He made no bones at all about knowing Miss Peters had been kidnapped.'

'Ah well, I told him that,' Mike admitted.

Rodgers raised his thick eyebrows and rubbed the flat of his hand on his bristly hair. 'Did you now? When?'

'This afternoon. We had a little chat at his place in South Audley Street. Quite a place, too. Have you seen it? Reminds me of a film set.'

The Inspector shook his head.

'Does he know that Jo's been found?' Linda asked.

'Yes, I told him,' the Inspector replied.

'How did he take the news – surprised?'

'Not unduly. He's pretty clever at concealing his feelings, I should say. Anyway, he's all yours. I've finished with him for the time being. I must be off now.' Just as he turned to leave he remarked, 'By the way, there are two friends of yours in the cocktail bar.'

'Really? Who?'

'Sanders and Miss Long. I don't know if they've been having a row or not, but things weren't too harmonious ten minutes ago. The lady appears to have had more than her share of the bottle.'

'Did you speak to them?'

'No. I was on my way to Corina's office. They didn't see me.'

'Did you make any progress with Saltoni, Inspector?'

'No, but I haven't finished with him by a long chalk. Excuse me, I have work to do.'

Linda finished the small amount of wine in her glass, then said, 'May I have this dance, Mr Baxter?'

Mike laughed and led her to the floor. 'You wouldn't be curious to know what's going on at the cocktail bar, by any chance?'

'Well, you must admit the evening's been a bit flat so far.'

The far corner of the dance floor was only a short distance from the bar. Never moving far away from one spot the Baxters were able to observe Irene Long and the Colonel for quite some time without being seen themselves.

'I rather fancy the Inspector was right,' Mike murmured

into his wife's ear. 'Irene Long looks as though she's got quite a load on.'

'Seems to make her bad-tempered into the bargain. The Colonel looks as though he'd dearly like to get rid of her.'

'Probably has been feeling that way for some time. I don't think Sanders is somehow the marrying type, and our friend Miss Long looks like a first-class case of *Torschluss Panik*, as the Swiss say.'

'What on earth is that?'

'Panic at the thought of the door being closed on them – in other words, of being left on the shelf. Wow! Listen to that voice of hers!'

Irene Long had slammed her glass on the top of the bar and her strident tones carried above the music. '. . . damn well get me another drink if I can't dance with Charles.'

'Irene, for heaven's sake pull yourself together!' Sanders exclaimed in a loud voice just as the music stopped. Looking round uneasily he caught sight of the Baxters. Embarrassment flooded his handsome, rather wooden features.

Mike and Linda walked up to the bar and they all exchanged greetings.

Irene Long said loudly, 'Isn't this hole deadly tonight?'

Sanders swallowed nervously and tried to bridge the awkward silence as people around them began to stare curiously. 'Irene's a bit upset about Corina not being here. She . . . er . . . prefers his style of dancing to mine.' His laugh was noticeably self-conscious.

'Victor, darling,' said Irene Long, 'you don't dance, you march from one corner of the parade ground to the other. For Pete's sake where's that gin I ordered?'

'No doubt Mr Corina will put in an appearance later,' Linda said.

'Later?' Irene Long cried, at least an octave too high. 'How much later can you get? It's nearly midnight, he ought to have been here hours ago! If Charles isn't going to dance with the customers they might just as well close the shop up.'

'It's too bad, isn't it?' Linda put in quickly. 'I was looking forward to a dance with him myself. Why don't you try my husband, Miss Long? He practically taught Fred Astaire all he knows!'

'Come off it, darling! I'm not that old,' Mike protested with a laugh, catching on to her idea. 'But if Miss Long cares to take a chance I'll be delighted.'

Irene Long shot him a look from under heavy eyelids which was meant to be coy. Its effect was partly spoilt by the fact that her eyes were unfortunately refusing to focus properly. 'You tempt me, Mrs Baxter. Your husband is a very attractive man. But I've already refused Victor . . .'

The Colonel was not slow in seizing his opportunity. 'That's all right, old girl, you go right ahead – the old legs have just about had it for tonight, anyway.'

Mike bowed and held out his arm to Miss Long. She took it in the grand manner, though a second later she seemed glad of it to prevent herself from stumbling. Mike steered her with great care between the tables and on to the floor. It was heavy going at first; she seemed about half a beat behind with all her reactions. Then she began to improve and by the end of the first dance their performance together was reasonably smooth.

As the music started once more he asked, 'Will you risk it again?'

She obviously welcomed the idea. By good fortune it was the cha-cha, one of the few dances Mike had really studied. So, apparently, had Miss Long.

When the number ended she let out a long sigh of satisfaction and regret. 'Your wife wasn't fooling, Mr Baxter,' she said breathlessly.

'You're no novice yourself, Miss Long,' he replied politely.

'And the quite heavenly thing is, you don't try and talk at the same time,' she added.

It was not until the fourth time round together that Miss Long, who did not approve of talking whilst dancing, began to do a lot of talking. Mike listened carefully and prompted her judiciously. It was just getting interesting when the music stopped and a cabaret interlude was announced. Inwardly disappointed, he led his partner, her eyes gleaming, back to the bar where Sanders stood waiting impatiently.

'I thought you two were going on all night!' he barked. 'Come on, Irene, we must be off.' Grabbing her arm and ignoring her protests he hustled her away.

Just as she was disappearing from sight she turned, caught Mike's eye, fluttered one hand limply at him, and shot him a scorching smile.

'Wow!' Linda exploded, trying to suppress her laughter and pretend to be furious. 'I hope there was a good motive behind that performance, Mr Baxter!'

Mike mopped his brow and grinned ruefully. 'Never worked so hard in all my life. But it was worth it. The guard came off her tongue.'

'Apart from any indiscreet suggestions, what did she have to say?'

'Two things of interest, one definite and one baffling. Definite is that when she said Hector Staines had never been to her flat she was telling the truth. I'm quite sure of it. Happily she brought the subject up, not I, so I don't think she suspected I was trying to pump her.'

'Did you get on to the subject of Nadia Tarrant?'

'No, and unfortunately she avoided it too. But here's the baffling thing: she gave me a cryptic sort of warning.'

'A warning? What did she say?'

'She said, "Whatever happens, don't go down to Reading." I told her I had no intention of going down there.'

'But why Reading?'

'God knows. I tried to press her but she just repeated those words and then she clammed up.'

'Do we know anybody at Reading?'

'Not a soul. I'll bear it in mind, though.'

Mike ordered a drink from the flaxen-haired bartender and then asked Linda, 'How did you make out with Sanders?'

Linda made an expressive gesture of exasperation. 'That is undoubtedly the dullest, most conceited, most crushingly boring ass I've met in a day's march. He has no more idea of the art of conversation than a stone Buddha!'

'Give the poor chap his due – he was probably pretty fed up at his girlfriend getting plastered.'

'Anyway, the only bright spot, apart from watching your intriguing exhibition on the dance floor, was the brief glimpse we both caught of Charles Corina.'

'Corina? He was in here?'

'He just put his head round the corner of the bar, back entrance, to give some instructions to that blond specimen there. He looked somewhat the worse for wear. I don't think he particularly wanted anyone to see him.'

'Too bad. Well, let's get our coats, we've got some visiting to do.'

'At this time of night? Where on earth are we going?'

'Reigate House, Chelsea.'

Linda opened her eyes wide and laughed. 'Darling, if you've

got a heavy date with your new girlfriend wouldn't you be better off without me?'

Mike put his arm through hers. 'Let's say I need a chaperon.'

Chapter Eleven

The caretaker of Reigate House was brewing tea and spreading sardines on a piece of toast when Mike pressed the bell of his basement apartment. They gathered through the badly fitting door that he was not very pleased to be interrupted; the tail-end of some solid North Country swearing accompanied his movements as he reluctantly came to the door.

'Yes?'

'Are you the caretaker?' asked Mike with careful deference.

'That's me. Dan Appleby.'

'Splendid, we are in luck!'

Mike beamed at Linda, who nodded, and flashed the portly caretaker a smile that would have melted butter on a cold plate. Even Dan Appleby's hostile stare seemed to thaw a trifle.

'You're not the bloke from Littlewood's, I suppose?' he said.

'From where?'

'The chap I've always dreamed about, the one that's going to knock on my door one day and tell me I've won the jackpot in the football pools.' He grinned and stared at them closely, finally shaking his head. 'No, I suppose that would be hoping too much. What d'you want?'

Mike had noted the war ribbons on the threadbare battle-dress blouse which the caretaker wore. 'In the Desert, were you?'

'Aye, Eighth Army,' the man answered with a glint of pride in his eyes.

Mike nodded, admiringly.

The caretaker opened wide the door to his cosy little den and ushered them in. Whilst Linda was made comfortable in a rickety wicker chair Mike encouraged him to talk about desert warfare for some minutes, until he felt he could judiciously steer the conversation round to the purpose of their visit.

'I'll tell you why I'm bothering you at this time of night, Mr Appleby. But I'd be obliged if you'd treat everything I tell you as strictly confidential. I want to make some inquiries about one of your tenants here.'

The caretaker's manner, which had thawed considerably during his recital of wartime exploits, became sharply suspicious. 'Are you working for the coppers, by any chance?' he demanded.

'The police? Good heavens, no! This is purely a private inquiry of rather an intimate nature, you understand.'

Mr Appleby got the message. Nodding sagely and giving Linda a knowing look he asked, 'Who's your client?'

'That's just it: I'm not sure what name he might be using. But perhaps you can tell me who occupies the flat alongside Miss Irene Long, and who is above her, or even below?'

Appleby thought for a moment, then answered, 'No one below, and the flat alongside is empty at the moment. People above are the Carbreeds, a Danish couple.'

Mike frowned. It was obviously not the answer he had hoped for. 'What do the Carbreeds look like?'

'Young, blond, both on the tall side. Nice people. They're not here at the moment. Gone back to Denmark for a few months, on a holiday.'

'And the flat? Is it empty during that time?'

'No, they sub-let. New chap's called Williams.'

Mike's interest quickened. 'What does he look like?'

Linda just gaped, but Mike nodded without surprise as Dan Appleby proceeded to give an unmistakable description of the elderly, limping, grey-haired Hector Staines.

'Is that the man you're after?' he asked, his eyes glinting with inquisitiveness.

Mike steered clear of the question. 'How long have you known this Mr Williams? Can you tell me anything interesting about his habits, where he goes, when he comes back, what he does for a living, if he has any visitors, and so on?'

Appleby could tell them little. The new tenant, it seemed, did not actually live in the flat but was content to use it at irregular hours a few times during the week, mostly during the evenings. On the whole he was quiet and well behaved, even if his movements had struck the caretaker as being a little odd.

Mike discreetly took out a note from his wallet as Appleby came to an end, and slipped it without ostentation under an ashtray on the table.

'You've been most helpful, Mr Appleby,' he said, rising from the creaking wicker chair that was blood-brother or even great-uncle to the one Linda sat in. 'My client is of a generous nature and will be most grateful for this information.'

Appleby's interest quickened at the sight of the note. 'Is there anything else I can do for you, sir?'

'Well, I hardly like to put you to any more trouble . . .'

'No trouble at all, sir.'

'I was just wondering if I might take a look at one of the flats? Of course, if you don't have the necessary authority I can always apply to—'

'I don't know about the authority but I've got a pass-key.' He winked heavily again at Linda. 'Was there any flat in particular you'd like to look over? Mr Williams's, for example?'

Mike gave him a conspiratorial smile and murmured, 'That would be very convenient.'

'Mike, I don't get it!' said Linda quietly whilst the portly Yorkshireman shuffled off in his battered carpet-slippers to fetch the pass-key. 'What's all this about a client? And why do you want to look at Staines's flat?'

'Our North Country friend has assumed I'm collecting evidence for a divorce case. We'll let him keep his illusions. As for Staines's flat, let's say I'm plain nosy!'

Dan Appleby shuffled back into the room holding the key aloft. He was whistling 'Twenty-one Today' softly and looked as though he were enjoying the midnight conspiracy enormously.

He took them up in the lift to the fourth floor and let them into Staines's flat. It had the dull, unwelcoming atmosphere of rooms not lived in, accentuated by the condition of neatness in which the few personal possessions had been left.

Mike surveyed the living-room critically. A hip-high radio baffleboard filled one corner of the room; the others were empty except for occasional tables and a standard lamp. He went over to the radio and moved it carefully away from the wall. Linda and Appleby watched with sharp curiosity as he inspected the few wires, traced their passage, shook his head, and returned the baffleboard carefully to its original position. An arm-chair thrust against one wall aroused his interest, but again the search proved apparently fruitless.

He found what he was looking for behind a heavy settee that ran the length of the wall opposite the fireplace.

As he pulled it clear he asked Appleby, 'Which room of Miss Long's is directly below this one?'

'Same as this – her living-room.'

Mike grunted and heaved the settee a foot from the wall to reveal a square metal box about the size of a small portable typewriter. He found a spring catch and flicked open the metal lid. He became aware of Dan Appleby breathing heavily over his shoulder.

'By gum, I reckon I know what that is, all right!' the caretaker exclaimed. 'That's one of them listening devices like we used to put in a Jerry prison camp to hear what they was saying.'

'You're right, Mr Appleby,' Mike said, unhooking a small set of earphones and examining the dials on the face of the case. 'No wonder Mr Williams only bothered to use this flat in the evenings; that would be about the only time there would be any conversation in the room below for him to listen to.'

'My God, the tricks people get up to nowadays, all in the name of Cupid! Life used to be a lot simpler in the olden days. I just hope my Missus doesn't get to hear of this; it might put ideas into her head.'

Mike glanced at Linda, who managed to keep a straight face, and replied. 'You're right, Mr Appleby. One cannot be too careful.'

'No wonder the old rake didn't want no cleaners about

the place. Insisted on doing all his own tidying up and everything. Slipped me a regular quid a week, he has, just to make sure I understood.'

Mike carefully replaced the listening-set in exactly the position he had found it and pushed the heavy settee back against the wall.

'Aren't you going to rip them wires out?'

'No, my client wouldn't want Mr Williams to know that we've tumbled to his . . . spying activities. For the time being we'll let him stay at his listening post. And I'm putting my faith in you, Mr Appleby' – he drew out his wallet and extracted a pound note – 'as a man of the world who understands the meaning of the words "tact" and "discretion", to say nothing about our little visit.'

The caretaker's grimy paw closed over the note with practised skill and he smiled broadly. 'You can rely on me, sir. And the more I look at you the more you begin to look like that chap from Littlewood's I'm always dreaming about.'

There was the sound of a door slamming below and footsteps crossing the room of Irene Long's flat. All three were instantly alert.

Appleby said in a hoarse stage-whisper, 'Reckon that'll be Miss Long. It's a woman's walk, by the sound of it.'

Mike smiled. 'You should have been a detective.'

'She's been quite a time saying goodnight to the Colonel, hasn't she?' Linda murmured.

Appleby led the way out and Mike said quietly to his wife, 'All the better for us. Let's hope she's sobered up in the meantime.'

Linda looked at him in astonishment and then glanced at her watch. 'Are we going to tackle her now?'

'I can imagine few more suitable occasions,' Mike replied in a grim voice.

Miss Irene Long found herself faced with a very different Mike Baxter from the smooth flatterer who had been with her only an hour earlier at La Pergola. She hesitated at the doorway and did not invite them in, but Mike simply thrust the door aside and strode into her flat. She tried to protest.

'Really, Mr Baxter, it's very late and I think I've had just about all I can take for one evening.'

'The evening's not over yet, Miss Long. Sit down.'

'But this is outrageous! I'm tired, I've got a splitting headache, and Victor made me drink far more than is good for me.'

'Rubbish! It isn't Sanders who is making you drink, Miss Long, it's your conscience, or plain fear. You're as sober as a judge now, though you'll have a cracking hangover tomorrow. Meantime I'd be glad to have a satisfactory explanation of that "warning" you gave me on the dance floor. What exactly did you mean when you told me not to go down to Reading?'

Irene Long sank into a chair, looking frightened and forlorn. She moistened her lips. 'I really don't know! My tongue must have run away with me. I didn't mean anything in particular.'

'Stuff and nonsense! I'm going to get this out of you if I have to stay all night.'

'I'll call the police,' she remonstrated, without much conviction.

'I doubt it. They're the last people you want to see.'

'Please, Mr Baxter, you must believe me . . .' Tears began to well up in her eyes and suddenly she looked her years,

145

no longer a smart and capable Bond Street saleswoman but simply a frightened and fading middle-aged blonde. Linda felt a pang of compassion for her but Mike was relentless.

'Spare me the histrionics – it's too late for that, in every sense.' He took a seat opposite to the weeping woman and looked her full in the face. 'In less than a week Harold Weldon will be hanged by the neck for the murder of Lucy Staines. A murder he did *not* commit. Are you going to sit here indulging in feeble hysterics whilst an innocent man goes to his death – an innocent man whom you might be able to save?'

'I . . . I need a drink.'

'No you don't! You've had your ration for one night.'

'Please leave me alone. I'm tired and upset. I want to go to bed.'

'What for? You won't be able to sleep. You'll get no peace of mind. Why not tell the truth? What do you know about the Weldon case? What are you hiding from the police, and from me? Why shouldn't I go down to Reading?'

She swallowed hard and said, 'I've told you all I dare. Please leave me alone.'

Linda caught Mike's eye and begged him to desist.

He nodded and stood up. 'Very well, Miss Long, if you won't play, be it on your own head. I've a hunch there's more trouble in store for you. But in return for your delivering a warning to me tonight let me also give you a warning: be careful what you say in this flat, in this very room.'

Irene Long raised her head and gave him a haggard look, the glimmerings of new fear dawning in her mascara-damaged eyes. Her voice was thin and shaky. 'What do you mean?'

'Have you ever seen the man who has the flat immediately above this?'

'Mr Carbreed?'

'No, he's back in Denmark with his wife. They've sub-let to a man called Williams. That doesn't happen to be his real name. It's Hector Staines.'

'I don't believe you.'

'Then ask the caretaker.'

Irene Long turned in desperation to Linda. 'Is this true Mrs Baxter? You wouldn't lie to me, would you?'

Linda was very pale and her voice carried utter conviction. 'Neither of us wishes to lie to you, Miss Long. We want to help you. You've got to be on your guard about what you say in this room because Hector Staines has wired it to a listening-set upstairs. He's been listening to all your conversations for quite a while. That's why he took the Carbreeds' flat.'

Irene Long opened her mouth to speak but no sound came – and for a very good reason. She had fainted.

Mike and Linda sat over a final night-cap in the lounge of their Sloane Street flat. They were utterly exhausted by the events of the day but strangely reluctant to go to bed.

'Why on earth do you suppose Staines wanted to keep tabs on her with his listening-set?' Linda mused.

'Not because she talks in her sleep, you can be sure of that. It must be her conversations with visitors, and who those visitors *are*, that interests Staines.'

'Poor old Irene Long,' said Linda. 'Do you think she'll be all right, darling? She looked pretty awful when we left.'

'She'll survive.'

'You can be very hard at times.'

'There are times when one has to be,' said Mike with a frown. 'The end justifies the means. Irene Long shouldn't have got mixed up in this business if she was scared of a few hard words now and then. She's lucky I didn't give her the full treatment, like someone handed Jo.'

Linda nodded in silent agreement.

'I'll give her a few hours to simmer gently,' Mike went on. 'After a ragged night she'll be ready to come to the boil . . .'

Chapter Twelve

The following day Mike made a careful examination of the two heavy books which had been sent by special delivery, and had just joined Linda in the lounge when the front door bell rang and Mrs Potter came in to say that Mr Corina wished to see him.

Charles Corina's manner, as he came into the room, was tense; he scarcely remembered his customary stiff little bow towards Linda, nor did he attempt to kiss her hand.

Uppermost in his mind, it appeared, was a recent encounter with Inspector Rodgers, and a brief and irritable account of it ensued.

'. . . There is nothing I detest more than being hectored by those bull-necked individuals,' he went on. 'I told him I'd report him to the Chief Commissioner of Police, and bring his behaviour to the notice of the Press.'

Mike shrugged. 'Rodgers probably thought he was just doing his duty, Corina.'

'Duty! The man's a sadist, an out-and-out ruffian! He should have been removed from the Force long ago. Just because he's too dim-witted to make any progress in his elephantine investigations there's no need to pick on me as a scapegoat.'

'Aren't you exaggerating a trifle?' Mike said quietly. 'I don't think Rodgers has much time for scapegoats.'

'Then why did he go on pestering me with all those silly questions?'

'For the simple reason that the unknown gang who kidnapped Jo Peters were apparently interested in one thing: why she was watching your night-club.'

'My club? But I'm the only person who would be curious about that!'

'Exactly,' Mike replied softly, watching Corina with great care.

Corina's unusually pale, agitated features froze into a stiff mask as he sought to gain control of himself.

Linda cut across the taut silence. 'Was that your only reason for coming to see my husband, Mr Corina?' she asked.

'No, not exactly. I saw Mr Baxter yesterday afternoon, and he asked me certain questions about a Nadia Tarrant . . . I'm afraid I lied to you,' he remarked blandly, turning to Mike. 'We all have our little vanities, and I'm afraid my pride would not allow me to admit that a woman like that had ever found her way into a place of La Pergola's quality.'

'So she *was* there! Who was she with?' Mike snapped.

'Irene Long, as you surmised.'

'Then why didn't you admit as much when we met yesterday?'

Corina pursed his lips, choosing his words with evident care. 'I'm afraid I could not. The circumstances were not appropriate. Since then things have changed.'

'Go on.'

'Do you think I might have a drink?'

Mike nodded and went to the drinks cabinet to comply with Corina's request.

This time he was rewarded with Corina's neat little bow; the man was clearly regaining his composure rapidly. He sat down, raised his glass to Linda, loosened the knife-like crease of his trousers at the knee, and began to speak.

'After I left the club last night I made a telephone call to an old associate of mine. You will observe that I use the word "associate", not "friend". The man's name is Westerman, and he was acquainted with Nadia Tarrant. In fact it was through Westerman that she contrived to gain admittance into La Pergola.'

He sipped his drink appreciatively.

'I think you ought to meet Westerman,' he went on. 'For a very small financial consideration he is prepared to tell you all about Nadia Tarrant and her association with Irene Long. He might even be persuaded to tell you about other matters which appear to have aroused your curiosity.'

'I see,' said Mike after a short silence. 'Do I take my cheque book or does he want crate-loads of bullion?'

Corina allowed himself a slight smile. 'That is something you will have to discuss with him yourself. I do not wish to be involved in the matter. I have delivered Westerman's message to you, and taken the liberty of arranging a suitable appointment for you. After that I wash my hands of the whole affair.'

'When am I supposed to meet him?'

'Tonight, at ten o'clock. Does that suit you?'

Mike glanced at Linda, who nodded slightly.

'All right. Where do we meet – here or at La Pergola?'

'Neither. I'm afraid you'll have to go out of Town. Not very far. Just to Reading.'

Linda suppressed an exclamation and at the same instant one of the empty glasses she had been collecting on a tray slid to the floor. Mike bent to pick it up, glad of the interruption whilst he collected his thoughts.

When he faced Corina again he was able to ask in a casual tone, 'Couldn't Westerman get up to London for an hour or so? It's not very convenient for me to go trailing all the way down to Reading at ten o'clock in the evening, you know.'

'I suggested that, but he wouldn't hear of it. I'll drive you down myself, to save you the bother.'

Mike appeared to consider the offer, then accepted.

'Right!' said Corina. 'I'll pick you up here shortly before nine. And please refrain from mentioning our arrangement to anyone.'

'I see. I'll go along with that if you'll give me a straightforward answer to a question. You lied about Nadia Tarrant, now I'd like to know if you were lying when you said you'd never heard of a Mr Bannister?'

'Bannister? No, I was being entirely truthful there. I've never met a man of that name in my life, so far as I can recall.'

'It could be an assumed name. How about this fellow Westerman?' Mike continued. 'What exactly do you mean by saying he was an associate of yours? Were you in business together?'

'Yes, we were. I use the past tense, you will note. We had what might be described as an agency. Only we fell out – a minor disagreement which should not have happened. After a while I went into business on my own and opened La Pergola. Then, some time later, I received a letter from Westerman telling me to come down to Reading.'

'Telling? Not asking?' Mike put in softly.

'That's his way. I went. He told me he wanted to make one or two friends of his members of my club. Two of them had already applied for membership but I had turned them down as they were not up to my standards. I wanted the cream at La Pergola, not the riff-raff. However, for certain reasons I had to do what Westerman wanted—'

'In other words, Corina, this Westerman had a hold on you. He was, in fact, blackmailing you?'

Corina looked uncomfortable, then shrugged his shoulders. 'In a way, yes. That was how Nadia Tarrant got into the club, and the fashion model crowd I'd been trying to avoid – Irene Long, Lucy Staines, Peggy Bedford, and so on.'

Linda smiled. 'Don't tell me Victor Sanders was a fashion model, Mr Corina?'

He glanced at her coldly. 'Victor Sanders is one of our original and most respected members, Mrs Baxter.'

'Peggy Bedford sounds as though she was a high-flyer,' Mike said, 'and maybe her pal, Lucy, was too, but Miss Long has always struck me as quite respectable.'

'Irene Long drinks,' said Corina shortly.

'Isn't that good for business?'

'Up to a point, yes. She goes beyond that point. The Americans have an ugly but expressive word for her type – a lush.'

'Was Harold Weldon one of your members?' Linda asked.

'No, but he came to the club once or twice. I forget who with.'

'Mr Corina,' Linda continued, 'you don't think perhaps this Westerman was using your club as a sort of headquarters? I mean, if he was mixed up with the Tarrant woman and—'

'That's exactly what I wondered, Mrs Baxter,' said Corina a shade too eagerly. 'I've also wondered if Westerman was responsible for kidnapping Jo Peters.'

'In other words, Westerman could actually be Bannister!' Linda suggested excitedly, glancing at Mike.

Mike did not seem to share her excitement at the idea and said stiffly to Corina, 'How about another straight answer whilst they're in fashion: who really told you Jo was attached to Scotland Yard?'

'Westerman,' answered Corina promptly.

'What exactly was this "agency" you conducted with him?'

'We imported and exported different products.'

'Drugs, for instance?' Mike shot at him.

Corina looked shocked. 'Drugs? Heavens no! Whatever put that idea into your head?'

'Because that's why Jo was watching La Pergola.'

Corina looked deeply perturbed.

Mike added, 'Scotland Yard suspected that your club was being used as a distribution centre. There was a trail that led across the Atlantic and seemed to end smack on your doorstep.'

Corina shook his head in bewilderment and rose to leave. 'The suggestion is absurd. I notice they have not felt strongly enough about it to bring any charges.' He looked at his watch. 'I must go, it is getting late and I have an appointment. I will call for you at nine o'clock tonight, then?'

'Very well. Nine o'clock.'

When Mike came back into the room after seeing Corina out Linda shot him an inquiring look. 'Well? How much of *that* are we supposed to believe?'

Mike sank down wearily on to the settee and held his head between his hands. 'It's a pack of lies from start to finish, if you ask me. There is no Westerman at nine o'clock tonight, and there never has been a gentleman by that name in the Weldon case. Corina is so fascinated by his intellectual superiority – and I admit he's nobody's fool – that he thinks the rest of mankind are gullible children.'

'Then Corina is the man we're looking for? Am I right?'

'I didn't say that, darling.'

'Now you're the one who's being evasive. Mike, who murdered Lucy Staines; do *you* know?'

'I think so.'

'Was it Harold Weldon?'

'No.'

'Did the same person murder Nadia Tarrant?'

'Yes.'

Linda paused, then went on carefully. 'That visit we made to the Reference Library – it was quite a lucky break, wasn't it?'

'You've studied the books then?'

Linda was staring at him, wide-eyed, her body tense. 'Darling – I think I know who it is!'

'Do you, Linda?'

'I'm afraid so. And I mean afraid. I'm scared. How could anybody be so . . . ruthless! What are you going to do next?'

Mike stretched, and slowly stood up. 'I'm not sure. But of one thing I'm absolutely certain. I'm *not* going down to Reading tonight!'

Mike spoke briefly on the telephone to Jo Peters, whose condition was still bad but by no means critical, and then he put in a more lengthy call to Superintendent Goldway at Scotland Yard and arranged for the delivery of a message to Harold Weldon at Pentonville. He could not afford to be too encouraging but he realised how desperately the man must be awaiting news of some kind.

Anxious to find out how Luigi Saltoni was behaving he

rang Inspector Rodgers's number but was told that the Inspector was out. Mike left word asking to be called back when Rodgers had a spare moment.

However, Inspector Rodgers did not telephone; he arrived in person a short time later.

'Hello, Inspector,' Mike greeted him. 'Would you care for a drink?'

'No thank you, Mr Baxter. I never drink when I'm on duty.'

'That must make you practically a teetotaller. I've never known you to be off duty yet.'

Rodgers smiled ruefully. 'Aye, it's a busy life. What's more, it shows no signs of getting any quieter. I've got three or four cases on my hands at the moment, all of them bearing the label "Top Priority" and "Most Urgent"! But I did have time to see Saltoni this morning.'

'How's his amnesia? Any signs of improvement?'

'None at all, I'm afraid. Whoever succeeded in cowing that weed into silence certainly made a good job of it. I'll have another crack at him tomorrow.'

Mike frowned. 'I have a feeling that he could tell us a great deal if only we could open his mouth for him. And there's probably some further useful information to be obtained from Jo Peters, too, only of course she's not shamming. But she's still too woozy to give a very coherent account of what went on.'

'Have you been to see her?' Rodgers asked.

'No, I decided not to after hearing her shaky voice on the phone this morning. I kept the conversation to a minimum.'

'And she gave us no new leads to work on?'

Mike shook his head and offered the Inspector a cigarette. Rodgers accepted with thanks and began pacing the room.

'I expect,' he said, rather abruptly, 'you'll find my attitude about the Peters girl rather callous. I mean, I'm sorry about the trouble she ran into, and all that, but if you'll forgive me for saying so, she did rather ask for it.'

Mike raised his eyebrows but did not interrupt. It seemed to him that the Inspector had something on his mind, and silence was the best way to help him get rid of it. As Mike watched the burly figure pacing up and down the room he tried to recall his exact first impression, only a few hectic days earlier, when Superintendent Goldway had quietly asked Rodgers up to his room at Scotland Yard. A keen, ruthless mind in a powerful body – he would have made a good lock-forward on a Rugger scrum – a man at peace with himself because of his single-minded devotion to his profession. All right, so far as it went, but was any pen-portrait as easy as that? All black and white, no greys at all? Had the man no other interests, no hobbies, mild vices, perhaps the odd weakness which would make him three-dimensional? Women, perhaps? Mike thought back, but could recall no single instance, no straying glance, no conspiratorial smile from man to man, no off-hand remark that could possibly suggest any such interest. Mike did not even know if the man was married. How about a weakness for money, or drink, or sartorial elegance, or big cars? With difficulty he restrained a laugh; such ideas were patently absurd. He came to the conclusion that he knew no more about Rodgers now than he had done the morning they had first met.

'Fighting crime is an ugly trade, Mr Baxter,' Rodgers was saying, 'and there's no room in the trade for light-hearted amateurs. I'm thinking especially of unprotected females. To be blunt, I take a poor view of the whole Jo Peters episode. It should never have happened.'

'I sympathise with you in a way, Inspector. It must be galling to have amateurs tripping over your feet all the time. I'm referring more to people like myself than to Jo, though. She's a bit above the amateur class, you know.'

'Nevertheless she's female and therefore vulnerable. If I'd known that she'd been instructed to watch La Pergola I'd never have gone near the damn place!'

'But her investigations had nothing whatever to do with the Weldon case, originally.'

Rodgers looked dubious. 'Are you certain?'

'Yes, Goldway told me. She was watching the club because it was thought it was being used as a drug centre.'

'That may be. But are you sure that has nothing to do with the Weldon case, and all that's happened in the last few days?'

'I begin to think there's nothing I can be sure about in the whole baffling mystery. What's your opinion?'

'I think the two are connected, Mr Baxter. Look at it this way: when Lucy Staines was murdered her shoe was missing.'

'That's true.'

'When Nadia Tarrant was murdered her shoe was also missing.'

'Go on.'

'In my opinion both these women were hiding something pretty valuable in their shoes. It stands to reason.'

Mike nodded. 'The same theory had occurred to me. But I'm not entirely convinced that the theory holds water. Look, I don't know if Goldway has told you the substance of Jo Peters's interrogation at the hands of those thugs?'

'He did finally decide to confide in me,' Rodgers replied sourly.

'Well, they put her through what amounts to a third

degree. But when she finally broke down and told them she was investigating a gang of dope-smugglers they seemed to lose interest in her and let her go.'

'And what does that prove?'

'Surely it's obvious. She wasn't concerned with their racket.'

'Never underestimate the enemy, Mr Baxter. It could have been a neat little bluff. It's possible you're thinking exactly what they want you to think. They question the Peters girl about her activities, learn she's on the track of dope pedlars, and then profess to be completely disinterested. They release the girl, knowing that she'll come straight to us with this bee in her bonnet that they've got nothing to do with such activities. It's a little too easy for my taste. I can't quite swallow it.'

Mike nodded thoughtfully. 'I hadn't looked at it in that light, I must say. It's quite an idea.'

Rodgers allowed himself the ghost of a smile. 'Oh, we do get ideas now and then, you know.'

'Let's take your idea a step farther,' Mike went on. 'How does Corina fit into the picture?'

'I'm prejudiced there, of course; he's a type I can't stand. But for my money, he's the head of the whole outfit.'

'And he murdered Lucy Staines?'

Rodgers scratched his bristly, close-cropped hair. 'I wouldn't go so far as to say that. It's possible that Harold Weldon was an associate of Corina's. We've checked up and proved that Weldon was seen at La Pergola a few times.'

'So Weldon actually did murder his fiancée?'

'I think so. Up till now there's not been a shred of evidence to the contrary.'

'What about Saltoni's statement?' Mike put in.

'You saw Saltoni. He's a weed that blows whichever way the wind's going. As a reliable witness no self-respecting Judge would listen to him for more than two minutes.'

Mike had to concede this point. For a long time he had realised that even if Saltoni stuck to his original statement that Nadia Tarrant was in his bed at the time she had claimed to have run into Weldon he would have a very hard time proving it. It would be Saltoni's word against that of a woman now dead; there would hardly have been any witnesses during the sordid little scene of love-making in his room at Meryl Street.

Mike's thoughts were interrupted by the ringing of the telephone and he lifted the receiver, murmuring an apology to the Inspector. Victor Sanders's voice boomed over the line. Mike listened and made an occasional comment; he had long ago learnt the uselessness of trying to get a word in edgeways with the Colonel in full cry. 'Hello, Sanders . . . Yes, that's right . . . Yes . . . I see . . . No, indeed I shan't . . . Thank you, Sanders, I'll remember what you say . . . Thank you, Goodbye.'

'Was that Victor Sanders?' Rodgers asked as Mike replaced the receiver.

'It was. Always makes me feel like a recruit with his buttons unpolished.'

'The fellow's a confounded nuisance!' Rodgers snapped. 'Hardly a day goes by without he's pestering me on the phone.'

Mike agreed. 'He's not my cup of tea either, but if ever I'm accused of murder I hope I have a staunch friend like that.'

'Just because he thinks his pal is innocent that doesn't entitle him to a halo.'

'No, but a lot of people think the way he does, without doing anything about it. Sanders is at least persistent.'

'If you ask me,' Rodgers growled, 'there are far too many people "doing" something about it. Everybody seems to want to get into the act. Sanders – Hector Staines – Miss Peters—'

'Mike Baxter?'

Rodgers's mouth twitched into a sour smile. 'Well, you said it first.' Mike laughed and Rodgers went on, 'I suppose that's rather churlish of me. I ought to be grateful for any help you can give us. But I'm a bit peeved about the Peters girl because I think the Superintendent ought to have taken me into his confidence earlier on. However, I suppose, strictly speaking, she wasn't working on the Weldon case.'

'May I ask you a question about Sanders?' Mike said. 'When you first described him to me you mentioned that he was a keen amateur photographer.'

'Yes, he's got photographs all over his flat, plastered on walls and ceiling practically. He's had exhibitions of his work in one or two galleries, you know.'

'I see. You don't happen to know if he develops them himself, do you?'

'I should imagine he does. Why?'

'Oh, I wondered, that's all,' replied Mike enigmatically, and switched the conversation. 'Inspector, forgive my asking, but are you married?'

Rodgers shot him a faintly startled look. 'No, I'm not. Why do you ask?'

'You spoke of vulnerability just now. No matter how tough we all like to think we are, we're all of us vulnerable through the women in our lives. Look what happened to my wife and me – or nearly did – when our car got shot to pieces in Darlington Street.'

161

'Yes, that was a near thing for both of you. But if anyone wants to take a crack at me they'll have to use the direct method.'

'And you don't think it's possible someone might want to do just that? Whoever's behind this mess, they're hardly using gloves,' Mike pointed out.

Rodgers shrugged his broad shoulders. 'It's possible, but danger is what I get paid for. There's nothing I can do about it.'

'You can be on your guard, though.'

'In what way?'

'Don't accept chance invitations,' Mike said, 'especially on the spur of the moment.'

Rodgers glanced sharply at him. 'Have you been getting any chance invitations?'

'Corina came here this morning and told me that a man named Westerman could give me – sell me – vital information about Nadia Tarrant and the Lucy Staines murder.'

'Westerman? I haven't heard that name before. Did he tell you anything about him?'

'Not much,' Mike replied. 'Apparently he lives in Reading. Corina suggested that he drove me down there this evening. I accepted the invitation, but I haven't the slightest intention of going.'

'Why not?'

'Because I'm convinced Westerman doesn't exist – the whole thing is just a trap.'

'Do you have any grounds for suspecting that?'

Mike nodded.

'You mean someone has warned you?' asked Rodgers.

'Yes, Inspector, and I'm warning you. Don't accept any invitations, especially from Corina.'

Rodgers rubbed his scalp with the palm of his hand. The sound was like the scraping of a soft shoe on a doormat. 'Wait a moment,' he said. 'If you fail to keep the appointment Corina's hardly likely to come to me with the same story.'

'On the contrary, I think that's exactly what he will do, and that's why I'm warning you. Work it out for yourself. If Corina thinks I've become suspicious about the idea he can hardly back out and pretend he never made such an appointment for me. Here's this man, Westerman, supposedly in possession of vital information concerning the Weldon case. If I don't bite, then Corina must logically pursue the matter, not climb down. He's quite likely to ask you.'

'Yes . . . perhaps you're right.' Rodgers grinned. 'But don't worry, Baxter. Forewarned is forearmed.'

When the Inspector had gone Mike took pen and paper and, after careful thought, wrote a short note and sealed it in an envelope addressed to Miss Irene Long, c/o Conway and Racy's. He handed the note to Linda and asked her to take it along personally.

'I'd ask Mrs Potter to do this errand,' he said, 'but this is rather like serving a summons. I have to be absolutely certain it's handed to the right person and Mrs Potter doesn't know her. Do you think you can find time on the way to your hairdressing appointment, darling?'

Linda nodded and tapped the envelope pensively in the palm of her hand. 'So you're putting on the pressure?' she queried.

'I've got to get quick results.'

'I hope you're right,' Linda said. 'Do I wait for a reply from Miss Long?'

'No, just say the note comes from me and that it's extremely urgent.'

'Right! See you later.'

Mike returned to his study and sank into the visitors' leather-upholstered chair to do some serious thinking. Unless he was very much mistaken his conversation with Rodgers had been a significant one. The Inspector was not a man to waste his words.

Mrs Potter brought tea, and eventually Mike attempted to do some work on the still uncompleted chapter of his book, but his mind was not on the job. It kept sliding off at a tangent, pursuing new permutations to the conundrum posed by Sanders, Staines, Irene Long, and Charles Corina. He was also, he realised, subconsciously anxious for Linda's return.

As five o'clock drew near and she had still not come back to the flat he found himself growing uneasy. His talk with Rodgers about a man's vulnerability through the woman he loves echoed grimly in his ears. As far as he remembered, Linda was due to be through at the hairdresser's at about half-past three. Such appointments tended to become protracted but he had never known her be as late as this.

At twenty past five, just as he was debating whether to ring the hairdresser's, the front door flew open and Linda burst in. Her hair, instead of looking immaculate, was dishevelled and there was a small strip of sticking plaster on her forehead. One hand was bandaged.

'Good God, Linda – what's happened?' he exclaimed.

'I'm all right, darling,' she murmured. 'It's nothing serious. I've been in a car accident, that's all.'

'That's all? For Pete's sake, how did it happen?'

'I was in Sanders's car.'

'*What!* Victor Sanders?'

'It wasn't his fault, darling. I'll tell you all about it in a minute. Ask Mrs Potter to fix me a strong cup of tea, will you?'

'Don't you want something a little stronger than tea, Linda?'

'Tea's the thing at a time of emergency. So British,' she added with a nervous little laugh. He could see she was more than a little upset.

When Mrs Potter brought in the tray Linda told Mike her story.

After handing Mike's note personally to Irene Long, Linda had gone into the restaurant next to Conway and Racy's and by chance bumped into Victor Sanders. They had exchanged a few words together and then gone their separate ways. But coming out of the restaurant later she caught sight of him a second time, this time from a distance, and as she emerged from her hair appointment later in the afternoon she had again run into him.

'You mean he was following you?' Mike demanded.

Linda's features crumpled in a frown. 'I don't know. Naturally I wondered if it could possibly be coincidence each time, but really I'm not sure he was following me. One often bumps into people one knows in Bond Street. And it's quite normal for the Colonel to be at Conway and Racy's, provided he and the girlfriend are still on speaking terms.'

'Yes, I got the impression he's rather attached.'

'My hair-do had taken longer than I'd expected, so although Sanders isn't exactly my type, when he offered me a lift home I accepted.'

Mike shook his head. 'It doesn't add up, darling. The

Colonel is no more fond of you than you are of him. I can't imagine why he should pursue you.'

Linda laughed. 'I swear I've got him sized up right – he conducts himself by a fixed code, with the title "How a Gentleman behaves towards a Lady", like something out of an Edwardian play. He doesn't see us as human beings, just as symbols of the Weaker Sex. He's actually a crashing bore but he thinks of himself as gallant; his code *demanded* of him that he offer to drive me home.'

'All right, but what about the accident? Was he hurt at all?'

'As a matter of fact he was pretty badly shaken up.'

'Which route did he take? Did it strike you as being the normal route?'

'Absolutely normal. The same thought passed through my mind – had it been a fixed-up job he'd probably have driven down some dark side-street, but he kept to the main road all the time. And he drove very nicely, I thought, no silly risks or anything. Besides if he'd planned to do me some harm he was taking a pretty big risk himself, wasn't he? I mean, it was this madman cutting in from behind us just after we'd come past the Palace who forced us off the road. Sanders was darn nearly killed!'

'These things can be simulated, by experts. What about safety-belts? Were there any in his car?'

Linda let out an exclamation. 'Exactly! That proves the Colonel's in the clear. I'd buckled myself in, as you always insist, but I'm pretty certain he didn't bother.'

Mike pursed his lips and offered Linda more tea, which she took gratefully. 'That's a point I'd like to be certain about before exonerating him. Now what about the car that hit you? Did you get a good look at it?'

'No, not very. I think it was a big American job – you know, one of those monsters with wicked-looking tail fins like can-openers. I was too shaken to get its number and by bad luck there were only a few startled Pakistani tourists who saw it, and we – that's to say the police – couldn't get much sense out of them. One thing I *am* certain of, the American job side-swiped us on purpose. There was absolutely no need to ride us off the road at that point; there was plenty of room.'

Linda sipped her tea and Mike was silent for a moment. Then he said, 'You realise what you're saying, don't you, if you insist that Sanders is in the clear? Someone must have taken a swipe at him. The fact that you were in the car at the time was pure chance, if your theory is correct. It's the Colonel they tried to harm.'

Linda nodded. 'In the taxi coming back, after I'd given my statement to the police, I thought the whole thing over carefully. I'm quite sure about it. It wasn't an accident, and it wasn't me they were after.'

Mike stood up and went to the window, staring out into the sunlit street. He glanced at his watch. 'When did it happen?'

'I'm not sure – about four o'clock maybe, or perhaps a bit later.'

'Then perhaps we'll be getting results from another quarter soon,' said her husband cryptically.

Linda gazed at him in bewilderment.

Ten minutes later the telephone rang. They exchanged a quick glance.

Linda opened her purse and took out a shilling. 'My money says it's Victor Sanders, ringing up to find out how I am. That's part of a Gentleman's Code.'

Mike produced a florin and placed it alongside the shilling. 'My money says it's a lady.'

He lifted the receiver. 'Baxter here . . . Yes . . . Yes, my wife told me . . . All right, the sooner the better. We'll be there in about twenty minutes.'

He hung up and swept the three shillings into his pocket with a triumphant smile. 'Irene Long wants to talk. My note worked! Come on, let's get cracking!'

Chapter Thirteen

During their short drive to Chelsea, Linda was in a bright, talkative mood, largely as a reaction from the mild shock of that afternoon.

Mike glanced at her worriedly, but decided it would be better to let her keep talking. Wild horses would not have prevented her from accompanying him now that the Weldon case looked like bursting wide open.

She went over her visit to Bond Street again for his benefit, describing Irene Long's reaction to his letter, then sat back with a sigh and said, 'Am I disturbing you with my chatter, by the way?'

'Not at all, darling.'

'Don't you want to think about what you're going to say to Irene Long?'

'I know what I'm going to say to her. One word: "Talk!"'

'Well, if I'm babbling too much just tell me to shut up. Let me see, where was I?'

Mike smiled. 'Just keep on babbling,' he said.

'As I was saying, life for Mrs Mike Baxter is pretty humdrum. A week ago she was stifling her yawns as she packed her clothes for a holiday in the South of France.

Happily no such frightfully boring event came to pass. Instead she has been shot at, nearly killed in a car smash, risked imprisonment for answering other people's telephones, and aided and abetted in the illegal search of a man's private flat . . . Have I forgotten anything?'

Mike laughed. 'I don't think so. Yes, you missed out Peggy Bedford. Hauling out bodies from gas-filled rooms has also been part of your deadly dull routine this week.'

'Exactly. Now the question is, should a wife stand for it? Hasn't a woman the right to live too? Why should we women be tied to the sink all day? You'd better watch your step, Mike Baxter, or I'm liable to go out hunting for a man who'll save me from this boredom and bring a bit of excitement into my life!'

'Perhaps Irene Long will do something to liven up the scene. After all, she was mildly entertaining the other evening with her little fainting act.'

'Gosh, I'd forgotten that. Add it to the list . . . To be serious for a moment, though – what exactly did you write in that note I delivered?'

Mike answered, 'It's not so much what I wrote that's frightened her out of her skin, it's what happened to the Colonel this afternoon. There's no doubt about her being pretty sweet on him, strange as it may seem. I simply told her that I know who Bannister is. As a matter of fact I was bluffing, largely because I'm not sure and I just hoped she'd spill the beans and confirm my suspicions. But the bluff seems to have paid off, in a way I didn't quite expect! I also mentioned that I'd spread the word around that it was Sanders who warned me not to go down to Reading. Now, it's my bet that when Miss Long heard about this afternoon's car smash she assumed that Bannister was behind it, and realised that her boyfriend is in grave bodily danger. I think that's what really scared her.'

'I'll have to digest that bit at leisure. My mind isn't working too smoothly at the moment. But one thing occurs to me; if we talk to her in her wired-up flat isn't there a danger of eaves-droppers?'

'A word with Dan Appleby and a little folding money should fix that. He can warn us if Hector Staines shows up.'

Irene Long sat bolt upright in a high-backed chair, her hands folded carefully in front of her, as though making an effort to retain the last vestiges of dignity as the humiliating story poured from her.

'I . . . I really don't know where to begin,' she faltered. 'When Lucy Staines first started work at Conway and Racy's I . . .'

'Suppose we start with the Cordoba robbery, Miss Long?' Mike put in firmly.

'The Cordoba robbery! You know about that?' She put her hand to her mouth in dismay.

'I've suspected for some time,' he replied. 'Go on . . .'

'But, Mike—' Linda began.

'Just a minute, Linda,' he interrupted her, and there was a moment of tense silence, Mike's gaze resting steadily on the pathetic blonde woman twisting nervously in the high-backed chair, before he spoke again. 'Some time ago a diamond pendant was stolen from a South American woman called Mrs Cordoba. She was staying at the Ritz, and the pendant – a cluster of rubies with three very large matching diamonds – was reported to be worth a quarter of a million dollars. The Yard investigated but the pendant was never recovered. Perhaps you'd like to continue from there, Miss Long?'

With some reluctance Irene Long took up the story. 'Mrs Cordoba was one of our best customers at Conway and Racy's. I sold her literally dozens of exclusive models. We got quite friendly and one day she invited me and two other girls to a cocktail party. We were rather excited about it and of course we accepted.'

'May I guess the names of the other two?' Mike put in. 'Peggy Bedford and Lucy Staines?'

'Yes. It was very glamorous and we had a good time. As a matter of fact, that's where I first met Victor Sanders. Charles Corina was also there – I think he'd played polo with Señor Cordoba out in Brazil somewhere. It was a memorable party in many ways. It was also the first time I saw the famous Cordoba pendant. Mrs Cordoba was wearing it.'

'Go on.'

'The next morning Lucy, Peggy and I naturally gossiped about the party during our coffee break. I didn't pay much attention to what Peggy said at the time, but afterwards I remembered her words very clearly. She said it was all wrong that a fat old harridan like Mrs Cordoba should be so rich and possess such beautiful jewellery. Jewellery of that quality ought to adorn the neck of someone young and pretty, she said, and of course she meant herself. She always did have her sights set a bit high. She said that if someone ever felt like taking Mrs Cordoba for a ride and relieving her of her jewel case, she – Peggy – would lose no sleep over it. Lucy and I laughed; we thought she was just making a joke.'

'Was Peggy Bedford acquainted at that time with Larry Boardman, or did that happen later?' Mike asked.

Linda interrupted Irene Long before the latter could

answer. 'Larry Boardman? That's the man whose photograph you found in Peggy's flat, isn't it?'

'When did she meet him?' snapped Mike.

'I'm not sure when she got to know Boardman. But a week after the party the pendant was stolen. Naturally we were all pretty excited at the news. I mean, having actually seen the pendant it gave us an extra kick. Anyway, soon afterwards Peggy was absent from work and she sent a note saying she'd been taken sick. Lucy was her closest friend and went round to see her. Peggy wasn't at home. She'd moved to a new address without telling us. Neither of us found this particularly unusual; she was rather a flighty young girl. She liked things to happen. "Action! Action! Let's have some action!" she was always saying. But what was unusual was her behaviour when she returned to work. She was quite out of hand at times, impertinent, wilful, almost arrogant. Something had turned her head. On one occasion I had to report her to the Manager, and as a result of this we fell out and didn't speak for several days.'

Mike lit a cigarette and offered one to Irene Long. She took it gratefully and drew on it deeply to steady her nerves. Mike sensed that she was bracing herself to tell of her own part in the affair and knew it wasn't easy for her.

'Some time later,' Miss Long went on, 'Peggy evidently decided she wanted to bury the hatchet. She invited me to dinner at her new flat. It was in Plymouth Mansions, where you found her body. Frankly, I was quite bowled over by the signs of luxury all round me. As you know, I live simply here' – she waved a hand round the comfortable, ordinary room – 'and officially I was earning a better salary than Peggy. But Peggy was clearly in the money. I was very surprised.'

173

'Someone who knew her has described Peggy Bedford as a high-class tart, Miss Long,' Mike interjected bluntly. 'In other words, a society call-girl. Are you suggesting that you were unaware of this side of her activities?'

Miss Long had winced at Mike's bluntness. She looked so unhappy at having to answer the question that Linda intervened. 'It doesn't really matter, does it, Mike? Let's leave it that Peggy suddenly came into the money. How did *she* explain this, Miss Long?'

'She said that a friend had died and left her three thousand pounds. She called it a pleasant little windfall. I pointed out that her windfall would soon disappear if she tried to live it up at that rate, but she only laughed and said there was plenty more where that came from. I didn't understand what she meant, but she wouldn't enlarge on the subject so I dropped it. Then, just as I was leaving, she gave me a parcel. "This is for you, darling," she said. "Just a little present to help patch up our silly quarrel." I took the parcel home, but I was too tired to open it until the next morning. You'll never guess what was inside that parcel . . .'

'I think I can, Miss Long,' said Mike dryly. 'A pair of shoes.'

Irene Long's eyes widened and she seemed momentarily at a loss.

Apparently ignoring her reaction Mike continued, 'And when did Peggy give Lucy Staines *her* present?'

Irene Long shook her head helplessly.

'But she did give Lucy a pair of shoes too, didn't she?' Mike persisted.

'Yes.'

'Were they the same as yours?'

'They were similar.'

Mike turned to Linda and explained. 'The Cordoba pendant was stolen by Larry Boardman, alias Leslie Bradley, alias a score of other names. It was common knowledge that he'd stolen it, that's to say the grapevine of the underworld knew it for a fact, but the police couldn't pin it on him. The most they could do was watch him. Of course, Larry Boardman realised he was being watched. He knew there was no point in trying to get rid of the pendant whilst the hue and cry was on. But a few months later he died. Before he died, however, he sent for a dear friend of his . . .'

'Peggy Bedford?' Linda suggested.

'He told her that the pendant was worth at least eighty thousand pounds. But he was too wily to hand it over. He told her that it must remain hidden for two or three years, until the heat was off.'

'But if Peggy didn't have the pendant . . . ?'

'She had something almost as good; a strip of microfilm showing the exact hiding-place.' He turned to Irene Long. 'Have I made any mistakes so far?'

She shook her head. 'No, it's all correct, though how you've been able to piece all this together I can't imagine.' Then, with a noticeable effort, Irene Long forced herself to go on with her sorry tale.

'At first Peggy didn't know what to do with the microfilm. I think it dawned on her that she'd bitten off rather more than she could chew. This was brought home somewhat forcibly to her when she got home one day and found her flat had been ransacked. She realised that other people were still actively interested in the Cordoba pendant; not only the police. She decided to cut the microfilm into three parts and she put each part into the heel of a shoe. I had one of the shoes, the second she gave to Lucy, and Peggy kept the third part herself.'

'Did you know about the film when she gave you the shoes?'

'No, it never entered my head. But she told me the whole story much later – just before Lucy was murdered, in fact.'

Mike nodded and was silent for a moment. Then he said, 'In view of all that's happened, don't you think you've been rather lucky?'

'Lucky? How do you mean?'

'Lucy Staines was murdered. Peggy Bedford also came to a sticky end. Nadia Tarrant was strangled.'

'I don't know anything about Nadia Tarrant.'

'You'd better think again, Miss Long. She was murdered and one of her shoes was also stolen. You met her once or twice at La Pergola. Saltoni saw you, and Corina himself confirmed it to me yesterday.'

The unhappy woman opened her mouth as if to contradict him, then thought better of it and with a heavy sigh continued, 'I sold my part of the film to Nadia Tarrant. How she found out that it was in my possession I never discovered. But I decided that some hard cash was preferable to the huge risk of hanging on to the film. She paid me a thousand pounds for it. After a while I decided I'd been foolish and had let it go far too cheaply, so I saw Nadia and . . . well, asked her for more money.'

'I think "put the pressure on her" would be a more exact description of your actions, Miss Long; even "blackmail" is not too strong a word. However, that is past and your dubious dealings have brought neither of you very much satisfaction. Tell me, was Nadia Tarrant buying the film for herself, or was she buying it on behalf of someone else?'

'She said she was acting as a go-between.'

'Did she name the other party?'

'No, she was much too cagey.'

'I see. Well, I imagine it's clear to you just how stupidly you've behaved in this matter. The moment you knew what was on that film you ought to have taken it to Scotland Yard.'

Irene Long gave a hollow laugh. 'It's easy to be wise after the event. If you've got any charity in you at all, Mr Baxter, which I doubt, you would understand how easily a person in my position can be tempted. I've always had to work hard for what I've got, and it seemed an easy way of making a quick thousand pounds. I couldn't see I was committing a very heinous crime. I hadn't stolen the pendant, and I didn't even keep the film.'

Mike shook his head reproachfully. 'The Lord protect me from feminine logic! Have you never heard of "aiding and abetting" – not to speak of your sordid attempt to blackmail the Tarrant woman? You *knew* what was on the film. No honest person would have had a moment's doubt about the correct thing to do.'

'I still count myself as an honest person, Mr Baxter. That was the only stupid action in my whole life. I was just too weak to resist the temptation, that's all.'

Mike eased himself out of his chair and walked over to the window, lost in thought. Miss Long shot Linda a beseeching look and watched Mike anxiously. Linda knew Mike would disapprove of any signs of soft-heartedness, but as she looked at the nervous wreck of a woman who had always been such a model of bright efficiency she felt a pang of pity surge through her. She was on the point of putting in a plea for Miss Long when Mike turned, his mind apparently made up. His voice was no longer so stern and relentless.

'I don't know how the police will look at it, but I'm prepared to do what I can to help you if you co-operate with me from now on,' he offered. 'I haven't forgotten that you did me a good turn by warning me not to go down to Reading. Since then I've received precisely such an invitation. I'm grateful for having been warned in advance.'

'Who invited you to Reading?' Irene Long asked.

'Corina. Didn't you know?'

'I was just coming out of the ladies' powder room at La Pergola when I heard two men talking outside. I didn't recognise their voices, but I heard enough of the conversation to gather they meant you some harm.'

'I see.'

'What do you mean by "co-operating" with you, Mr Baxter? Just what is involved?'

'Nothing very strenuous. I just want you to give a cocktail party. At my expense, of course.'

Irene Long blinked with surprise and looked relieved. 'When?'

'Tomorrow evening. Here, in this flat.'

'All right. Whom do you want me to invite?'

'Everybody who's had anything to do with the Weldon case. Victor Sanders, Hector Staines, my wife and me, Inspector Rodgers, and Superintendent Goldway.'

'Will they come?'

'That's up to you. I rely upon your persuasive powers to see that they're all here. As you don't know Goldway I'll arrange that. But you're responsible for all the others. Is that clear?'

'You did say cocktails? That means it would be fairly early?'

Mike considered briefly. 'Say, seven o'clock. Oh, one more guest. I think you'd better invite Charles Corina.'

She nodded without speaking, then Mike picked up his hat and, taking Linda's arm, left the room.

Chapter Fourteen

By no stretch of the imagination could Irene Long's cocktail party the following evening have been described as a jolly occasion. Despite their hostess's liberal hand with the cocktails not one of the guests seemed able to relax. Linda's description of the party, delivered privately to her husband afterwards, was that it had reminded her of a group of rival bidders at an auction, each stalking the others suspiciously round the room, each fearful one of the others might steal a sudden advantage.

There were eight people in the room – eight people and one who was only there in spirit: the one who had brought them all together. On the outcome of the party depended whether he would leave Pentonville alive.

Irene Long did her best. Darting to and fro with a forced smile on her heavily made-up face and the cocktail shaker in her hand she tried in vain to get the various groups to mingle. Superintendent Goldway and Inspector Rodgers made a stubborn pair near the door, the latter looking a trifle uncomfortable in a stiff white collar and a dark suit, too tight for him, which he clearly detested having to wear. Victor Sanders glared suspiciously at all and sundry from a lone post near the drinks cabinet, which he evidently judged to be the sole tolerable position in the room. Charles Corina was assiduously applying his Continental charm on an uneasy Hector Staines by trying to talk to him about some of the nondescript pictures hanging on Irene Long's walls, but it was obviously heavy going. The Baxters sat on the settee, at ease with themselves like two contented theatre-goers waiting for the curtain to go up.

It was Victor Sanders, red-faced and testy, who raised the curtain. 'Look here, Baxter,' he barked in an ear-cracking voice that brought instant silence, 'I wish you'd put me in the picture! What the devil's all this in aid of?'

Mike pretended wide-eyed innocence, at the same time trying to suppress a smile as Linda murmured in his ear, 'Smartly to attention when you're spoken to.'

'Miss Long thought it would be nice if we could all get together for a little chat, that's all.'

'My good man, we're not children, you know. It's perfectly obvious you're the one who dragged us here this evening, not Irene. She looks ready to drop. I can't imagine why she allowed herself to be talked into such a scheme.'

This was true. Irene Long looked haggard. No amount of cosmetics could hide the drawn lines of her face, the dark rings under her eyes. She began with a nervous laugh, 'Please, Victor—' but Corina cut her off.

'I must confess I tend to share Mr Sanders's views. Are you just indulging your talent for melodrama, Mr Baxter, or perhaps you are short of material for your crime stories?' He gave a thin smile, his eyes glinting with the prospect of verbal fencing to come. He seemed very sure of himself.

181

'If I were,' Mike answered, 'the Weldon case has certainly provided me with plenty of food for thought.'

'Have you something to tell us, Mr Baxter?' Staines said unsteadily. 'If so, I wish you would get on with it.'

Mike fixed him with a narrow-lidded stare and Staines shifted uncomfortably on his feet and looked away. 'Someone in this room has something to tell us, Mr Staines. I'm waiting for him to speak up. Let me refresh his memory: in May this year Lucy Staines was murdered, and her fiancé, Harold Weldon, was arrested and convicted of the crime.'

'It was a false conviction!' Sanders put in hotly. 'Harold was not the murderer.'

'Correct. He was not.'

'Perhaps you would like to tell us who did it, Mr Baxter?' Corina suggested with a trace of irony.

'We'll come to that in a few moments. Have patience. It is true that Weldon did have a row with Lucy. Mr Staines and others heard them. But in view of the fact that Weldon did *not* subsequently carry out a murder this quarrel has no significance whatsoever. We can forget it and look elsewhere for the motive and the killer. The seeds of that motive are to be found in a photograph of a well-known jewel-thief, which I found in Peggy Bedford's flat after her death.'

'Larry Boardman, I take it you mean?' put in Goldway.

Mike nodded his agreement. 'Otherwise known as Leslie or Leonard Bradley at the time he was friendly with Miss Bedford. The grapevine of the underworld credited Larry Boardman with the theft of a valuable piece of jewellery – the Cordoba pendant. I believe the police knew this too, Inspector?'

Rodgers made a sour grimace. 'We knew of it, yes, but we didn't have enough evidence to pin it on Boardman. We were watching him, then suddenly he died; of natural causes, strange to say.'

'Exactly,' Mike went on. 'But just before he died Boardman gave his girlfriend, Peggy Bedford, a strip of microfilm which indicated the hiding-place of the Cordoba pendant. Several attempts were made to get hold of the film, and in desperation she cut it into three parts and hid each part in the heel of a shoe. Realising she was still sitting on something too hot for her, she gave away two of those shoes—'

Staines cut in excitedly, 'To the two girls who got killed, Lucy and Nadia Tarrant!'

'To Lucy, yes, Mr Staines. But not to Nadia Tarrant.'

'Just a minute, Baxter,' Sanders interrupted, putting down his glass and advancing towards the settee. 'If the Tarrant woman did not have one of the shoes then she did not have one third of the film!'

Out of the corner of her eye Linda caught a glimpse of Irene Long holding unsteadily on to the mantelpiece. She wondered if Sanders was thinking at that precise moment of his abortive telephone call which she, Linda, had answered.

Mike answered imperturbably: 'I simply said that Peggy Bedford didn't give it to her. But Nadia Tarrant *had* a third of the film, because she'd managed to buy it from . . . someone.'

'Who would that be, Mr Baxter?' Rodgers asked patiently. 'Surely not from Lucy Staines?'

'No. Someone who shall be nameless, for the time being, at any rate.'

Corina broke the taut silence. 'May I ask the chairman of this little meeting a question? Where does the elusive Mr Bannister fit into the picture? You have professed a keen interest in this mysterious gentleman.'

'My interest is as keen as ever, Corina. The unknown gentleman passing himself off under the name of Bannister knew that Larry Boardman had given Peggy the microfilm. He was determined to get it, cost what it may. He commissioned Nadia Tarrant, who was no plaster saint, to buy one of the pieces of microfilm. Then Bannister murdered Lucy Staines—'

'You're quite sure about that, Mike?' Goldway inquired anxiously.

'Quite sure. And a few months later he faked the Peggy Bedford incident to make it look like suicide—'

Staines gave a cry of surprise. 'Do you mean Peggy was murdered?'

Everybody in the room gazed at him, stunned by the vehemence of his reaction and by the unexpectedness of Mike's statement. Staines was plainly taken aback; he was gripping his stick as though on the point of lashing out at someone. With a flash of feminine intuition Linda became absolutely certain that the old man had been desperately in love with the murdered girl, despite the difference in their ages and the dubious quality of Peggy's background.

Goldway said quietly, 'I must ask you again, Mike – are you quite certain you've got your facts right?'

'That's a statement of some consequence, Mr Baxter,' Rodgers added. 'I hope you've weighed up the possible insinuation of your remark?'

Mike nodded calmly. 'Let's leave the details till later, and continue our examination of the movements of Mr Bannister. He now had two pieces of the film, and Nadia Tarrant had managed to buy the third piece for a thousand pounds. As soon as she handed over the third strip he would have what he wanted – knowledge of the hiding-place of the Cordoba pendant, a cluster of diamonds worth eighty thousand pounds. He must have thought he was nicely home . . . But his ship ran aground – stuck on the reef of a woman's greed: Nadia Tarrant refused to hand over. She wanted a share of the profits too. "When thieves fall out . . ." There was only one way of getting his ship under sail again. He had to murder Nadia Tarrant. He lured her into meeting him at a quiet spot in some woods near Farnham, whilst at the same time arranging for an impersonator to dress up like Miss Tarrant and search her digs in Soho Square.'

Sanders boomed, 'Then this swine Bannister, whoever that is, faked the evidence against poor old Harold?'

'Of course. He primed Nadia Tarrant with photographs of Weldon so that she would know what he looked like, then when Weldon was accused of the murder she had no difficulty in picking him out at the police identification parade and claiming that she'd seen him running away at midnight from the scene of the strangling. The rest of the evidence wasn't hard to fake, and he made a very neat job of it. Weldon played into his hands by his open quarrel with Lucy and by making a false statement about his alibi to the police.'

There was a strained silence, in which Inspector Rodgers lit himself another cigarette and Corina strolled casually over to the drinks cabinet to pour himself another cocktail. The cabinet was placed against the wall in one corner of the room, so that Corina faced them all as he turned round and said pleasantly, 'A fascinating tale you make of it, I must say, Mr Baxter. Have we indulged your sense of drama sufficiently to be told who, in your opinion, is this mysterious Mr Bannister?'

Mike eyed him narrowly. There was no trace of sound in

the room except Staines's heavy breathing and the slight tap of glass on wood as Corina placed his glass on a ledge of the cabinet and relaxed in an attitude of gentle mockery.

'Perhaps you'd like to answer that for us, Corina?' Mike said in a level voice.

'You flatter me. Whatever makes you think I am in a position to answer your clever little conundrum?' He smiled and reached for a cigarette in an open box near by. With his other hand he felt for his lighter. But it was not a lighter that he held when he finally withdrew the hand from his pocket. It was a compact but deadly-looking revolver.

'Look out, Baxter!' Rodgers shouted, and both women screamed. Sanders made an instinctive movement but Corina whipped the gun towards him and rapped out, 'All right, the party's over, there'll be no more games. Everyone back up against that wall . . . go on, quickly now! Rodgers, Goldway, get away from that door, I'm going now and I don't want to have to shoot my way out!'

Somewhat sheepishly they obeyed him, stumbling into line along one wall, leaving a clear passage for Corina to walk down the room and out of the door. He passed rapidly down the line, the gun poised in one hand and the other making a brief but effective search for concealed weapons. No one was armed.

Just as he was leaving he caught sight of Linda's handbag. He snapped open the clip and tipped the bag upside-down. spilling the contents on the carpet. He smiled at Linda, 'Women have been known to play about with these things,' he said, indicating the gun in his hand. 'I shall lock the door from outside. The first person who tries to break through will get a bullet in the chest. That's about all, I think.'

He took the key from the lock, backed swiftly through

the door, and in a second had locked it behind him. There was no further sound.

Sanders was the first to make a move. The Code of a Gentleman called for it. Swearing something about 'damned swine' he made a move towards the door. Irene Long screamed at him, but Inspector Rodgers reassured her. 'He's hardly likely to be lurking outside. First thing he'll do is put as much ground between us and himself as possible.' He wheeled and made for the telephone but Goldway had got there already and was just finishing dialling. A second later he was issuing instructions for a general alarm to pick up Charles Corina, proprietor of La Pergola night club, Hampstead.

When he had finished Sanders had taken off his coat and was brandishing a poker, with which he proceeded to attack the door lock noisily, but not very effectively.

Mike restrained him. 'Steady on Miss Long's paintwork, old chap! I think there's an easier way.' Turning to Hector Staines, who was sitting down on the settee looking old and tired, Mike asked, 'I believe the caretaker has a pass-key. You don't happen to know Dan Appleby's private number, do you?'

Staines blushed scarlet and muttered some unintelligible answer, whilst Rodgers and the others looked puzzled. Irene Long recovered sufficiently to supply the number and a few minutes later Dan Appleby opened the door with his pass-key and did a double-take when he saw the motley group inside Miss Long's flat. His face was such a battleground of vast curiosity, blank surprise, and instant recognition of the Baxters that Linda could not repress a smile.

Under cover of the confusion Mike was able to draw Goldway to one side and murmur quietly, 'A word in your ear, John, when you have a spare moment. Preferably somewhere very private.'

Goldway flashed him a sharp, understanding glance and muttered, 'Be at my house in one hour.'

Twenty-four hours later Mike let himself into his flat and was greeted by an anxious Linda.

'Darling, Inspector Rodgers was here only a moment ago. There's no news of Corina. You don't think they're going to bungle it after all your hard work, do you?'

Mike smiled. 'I don't think they're going to bungle it.'

'I hope you're right. How did Weldon take the news?'

'He was slightly less sarcastic than usual. He actually thanked me! I told him it was the Home Secretary and Goldway that he had to thank, not me.'

'You're too modest. Is that all he had to say?'

Mike chuckled. 'No. One has to admire his spirit, considering the hell he's been through. When I told him about the reprieve he said, "How very convenient; now I can take my lawyer his cheque in person, and tell him what to do with it."'

Linda laughed, and then her tone became serious. 'It's all very well, but I still don't understand why it should take the authorities so long to pick up Corina. Inspector Rodgers told me they've got all the ports and railway stations and airports sealed and scores of men out on the job. He himself doesn't look as though he's had a wink of sleep in ages.'

'I don't suppose he has. Now stop worrying, Linda. I promise you everything's going to be all right.'

The telephone rang and Linda answered it. She handed the receiver to Mike. 'It's John Goldway for you, darling.'

'Mike here, John . . . Yes, everything's under control . . .

I know he has, but he'll keep this appointment, I'll bank my life on it . . . Quite. The main thing is to be sure the place is *completely* surrounded, but your men must keep out of sight . . . Thank you, John. Nine o'clock on the dot.'

As he replaced the receiver Linda broke in excitedly, 'An appointment with Corina? Where?'

Mike placed two fingers under her chin and smiled at her. There was a glint of anticipation in his eyes as he answered, 'Where is Charles Corina generally to be found at nine o'clock in the evening? At La Pergola, of course.'

Linda was about to ask more questions but he cut her short. 'Now be a good girl and find a nice book and curl up on the settee for a short while, will you? I shan't be long.'

'Where do you think you're going?'

'To La Pergola, of course.'

'Without me?' Linda asked in astonishment.

'Darling, there's just a chance this could be a bit of a rough house. Not what I'd describe as a ladies' night.'

'Not a hope, Mike Baxter! I'm not leaving the race just as we're reaching the finishing post. You'll have to tie me down if you want to leave without me!'

Mike looked at her and slowly shook his head. 'And this is the woman who was complaining only yesterday – or was it the day before – that her life was dull. I ask you!'

At La Pergola Club Linda failed to notice anything unusual except that the place seemed very full. The same sinuous brunette with the startling cleavage who had been huddling over the microphone on their first visit to the club was again moaning what sounded like exactly the same song; the same brand of pasty-faced débutantes and chinless young men were drifting listlessly in the soft-focus lighting on the tiny dance floor to the music of the small Latin-American band. Pink-jacketed wine waiters glided with their customary skill in and out of the tables, and the flaxen-haired bartender still badly needed a haircut. Linda was so keyed up she was unable to hide her disappointment.

Mike reproved her in a low voice. 'What did you expect, Linda – blue helmets peering out from underneath each table and the Police Band up there on the stage instead of our Latin American friends?'

'But I didn't see any of Rodgers's men outside either.'

'You weren't meant to. But they're there, have no fear.'

'What on earth makes you think Corina will come back here, of all places in the world?'

'Let us say, exactly because it's the last place in the world where he might be expected.'

Linda looked at him sharply. Despite the easy, almost flippant manner in which he had answered her questions, she knew him well enough to be able to detect the signs of unmistakable tension beneath the surface as his eyes flickered swiftly round the crowded room. She caught her breath as she saw Inspector Rodgers seated alone at a table in an alcove from where he commanded a good view of the packed room. She nudged Mike but he cut short her comment.

'I know, I've seen him. Don't do any handstands. I'll just have a brief word with him, then I'll join you at the bar. John promised to meet us here at nine o'clock. And if there's a rough house dive under the bar.'

He waited a moment until he saw Linda safely seated at the bar, then turned and made his way towards the Inspector's table. Rodgers rose and greeted him in a voice strained by fatigue. They both sat down.

'Any sign of Corina yet?' Mike asked.

'No such luck. What are you drinking?' Rodgers signalled a waiter and ordered a dry martini for Mike and a tomato juice for himself. He grinned self-consciously and added, 'I'll take my first tot when we've rounded up our man, and believe you me it'll be a stiff one!'

Mike smiled. 'I'll bet it will. Cigarette?'

Rodgers accepted, chain-lighting it from the one he had nearly finished. He said, after he had inhaled deeply, 'Tell me, what made you so sure it was Corina at the bottom of all this?'

Mike raised his eyebrows. 'You mean you didn't suspect him?'

'Oh, he was a suspect all right, but not at the top of my list.'

'Who was, if I may ask?'

'Harold Weldon, I'm afraid. Later, after the Peggy Bedford incident and the Tarrant murder, I had to think again.'

'And you settled on . . . ?'

'Victor Sanders.'

Mike nodded. 'Logically enough, I must say. Sanders was friendly with both Irene Long and Harold Weldon. His girl-friend had one third of the microfilm; all Sanders had to do was to get the second part from Lucy Staines—'

'And he'd be two-thirds of the way home.'

'Exactly. That left Peggy Bedford with the missing third.'

'Yes.'

'Weldon, however, wouldn't play. So Sanders decided to enlist the services of Hector Staines; he ought to be able to get it for him from his daughter. He told Staines about the film and promised to cut him in handsomely on the proceeds. Staines was always chronically hard up, part of the trouble being that he was trying to make the running with a very

191

expensive young lady – Peggy Bedford. It costs money to court a young lady of her tastes. Unfortunately for Sanders and Staines, Lucy was murdered before they could get at her.'

Rodgers nodded. 'And we don't need to ask who killed her.'

'Naturally, it was the mysterious Mr Bannister, who knew about the Cordoba robbery, knew about Larry Boardman, and knew that the hiding-place of the pendant was indicated on a strip of film which had been cut into three pieces. He also knew that Lucy Staines had one of them.'

The waiter arrived with their drinks and Mike sipped his appreciatively. 'Staines was of course horrified by the death of his daughter, but I don't think it came as such a shock to Victor Sanders. He already knew quite a lot about Bannister and realised he must be the murderer. That's why it shook him so rigid when his friend, Harold Weldon, was arrested and convicted. Sanders learnt of the Fairfax entry in Lucy's diary and came to the conclusion that Fairfax was another name for Bannister. That was why he concocted that letter from a mythical Fairfax, intending to show that Weldon had been framed, which indeed he had.'

'By Bannister?'

'Yes, by Bannister.'

'My first impression of both Staines and Sanders,' Mike went on thoughtfully, 'was moderately near the mark. They were both genuinely anxious to prove Weldon's innocence, but as their own hands were far from clean they couldn't press the matter too hard.'

'Yes, that adds up,' Rodgers commented. 'But tell me, where do you think the Tarrant woman fits into the picture?'

'She was bought and paid for by Bannister. He told her

to get hold of Irene Long's portion of the microfilm. She succeeded in this, but Sanders got to hear of it and was furious when he heard that his girlfriend had got cold feet and had sold out for a mere thousand pounds. That's a pretty small share of a pendant worth fifty thousand.'

'So he immediately offered the Tarrant woman fifteen hundred?' Rodgers suggested.

Mike nodded. 'Something like that. I don't know the exact figure. But that's what he was telephoning about the day Linda and I were in that ghastly dump in Soho Square. He said, "What about the Bannister affair; do I get the third shoe?" – by which he meant the third piece of film.'

'H'm. We all know what happened to Nadia Tarrant.'

'Yes, but she was the sort of person one could very easily underrate.'

Rodgers glanced at him sharply. 'How do you mean?'

'Even a man of Bannister's class underrated her,' Mike replied.

'I don't quite get that.'

'He must have paid her a substantial sum to testify against Harold Weldon.'

Rodgers nodded thoughtfully. 'Unless he was blackmailing her, of course. In which case it wouldn't have cost him anything.'

Mike conceded this point. 'True enough, but it's my belief she was on the point of blackmailing him.'

'How? She'd never actually met him, had she?'

'No. She didn't need to. She had her suspicions and she made a few inquiries in the right quarters. She even went to a Reference Library.'

Rodgers's brows knitted in perplexity.

Mike smiled and enlarged on the statement. 'It's a library

just off Tottenham Court Road. She looked up the person she was suspecting in a weighty reference book. I imagine she must have found out certain things about the mysterious Mr Bannister and she wanted to check them against the biography of the person she thought was Bannister.'

Rodgers stubbed out his cigarette and lit a fresh one. His tomato juice remained untouched. 'You seem to have dug up a surprisingly large amount of information in the past few days. A pity we haven't got you on the Force, Mr Baxter.'

'That bit wasn't difficult. Luigi Saltoni said they met in a Reference Library, which struck me as rather odd. I went there a day or two ago and found out that Nadia Tarrant had asked for two books. One was a hefty tome called *The Theory of Photographic Process*.'

'That's interesting! Sanders's pet hobby is photography.'

Mike nodded. 'Yes, but it was the second book she was really interested in. It was called *An Encyclopaedia of the Social Sciences*. You'll know the one I mean.'

Rodgers's eyes narrowed but he made no comment.

After a pause Mike went on, 'It contains a large number of biographical details about CID personnel.'

Rodgers stiffened, but his face was a blank mask. 'Rather an odd place to look for Charles Corina, wasn't it?' he said at length.

Mike leaned across the table and said quietly, 'Nadia Tarrant wasn't looking for Corina. She was interested in the biography of Detective-Inspector Rodgers.'

Rodgers seemed amused. 'Are you saying that this Tarrant person suspected *me*? She thought *I* was Bannister?'

'That is what I am saying.'

'But for Pete's sake – why?'

'Because you *are* Bannister, Inspector,' Mike ground out savagely. 'That's why!'

Rodgers stared at him in blank and utter astonishment. 'What in heaven's name are you driving at?' he said at last.

Watching Rodgers's hands, Mike went on deliberately, 'Shall I tell you why you came here this evening, Inspector?'

'To get Corina, of course!'

'No, not to get him, but to meet him. Corina sent you a note, telling you to meet him here, adding that if you failed to turn up he would be forced to put certain uncomfortable facts on Superintendent Goldway's desk tomorrow morning.'

Rodgers's expression changed almost imperceptibly, but there was a fine controlled sarcasm in his voice as he retorted, 'How very enlightening! Do go on.'

'You were prepared to do a deal with Corina,' said Mike flatly.

'Nonsense! If I were really Bannister I wouldn't need to do any deal with him. I would presumably have the whole film.'

'You have. All the three sections are in your possession, but Corina knows too much. You need him out of the way, then your road is clear. You let the Cordoba affair die down, bide your time, pick up the pendant, and quietly disappear.'

'Baxter, you're out of your mind!'

'No, I'm inside yours, Rodgers. I happen to know you received that note from Corina because I was there when he wrote it and I actually posted it myself. If you don't believe me, ask Corina.'

For the first time Rodgers was visibly disconcerted. He seemed to bunch together like a coiled spring. 'And where might Corina be?' he rasped.

'He's standing right behind you, Inspector.'

Rodgers whirled round, his full glass of tomato juice in his hand. 'Blast you, Corina!' he yelled, and flung the contents into Corina's face, at the same time lunging out with his feet and upturning the table as Mike jerked forward to grab him. Mike was sent sprawling, a woman screamed, and in a few seconds utter confusion reigned in the room. Rodgers vaulted with incredible agility across the alcove, aimed a savage kick at Corina's groin, and shot out of sight down a thickly carpeted corridor.

Mike staggered to his feet, jumped over the railing, and crouched at Corina's side. 'Where does that passage lead to?' he shouted above the din.

'My office,' Corina muttered, clutching his stomach.

'Anywhere else?'

'No, it's a dead end.'

Mike jerked upright and found Goldway by his side.

'Mike! I was watching, but I wasn't quite quick enough. Are you hurt?' Mike made a move in the direction of the corridor but Goldway held him back. 'I've got men stationed all over the place, leave this to us.'

His words were cut short by scattered gun-shots, and a second later a sergeant in uniform ran up, clutching his shoulder. 'I was waiting in the passage, sir, but he shot his way past me. He's locked himself in the office. I think I heard the window sash going down. Poulson and the others must have got him from below as he tried to climb out.'

Mike pushed his way roughly through the dazed crowd and reached the exit. Vaguely he realised that Linda was close behind him.

Outside in the street a small knot of bystanders and a large number of police were gathered in a half-circle round the body that lay in an ugly sprawl on the pavement beneath the open window. A police doctor thrust his way through the onlookers and knelt at the side of the body.

The pink-and-blue neon sign flickered on and off, casting an unholy radiance on the half-circle as the doctor straightened up and snapped his medical bag shut with unmistakable finality.

Chapter Fifteen

At the Baxters' flat, two hours later, they were praising Mrs Potter's coffee, and Mrs Potter, beaming with pride, had gone to make some more.

'You can't leave yet, John,' Mike said. 'Linda's simply bursting with curiosity.'

'There is one thing I don't quite understand,' Linda began plaintively, but was halted by the burst of laughter coming from both men.

'There you are, you see!' Mike teased her.

'What is it that you don't quite understand, Linda?' asked Goldway.

'Well, for one thing, why did Rodgers, or Bannister, or whatever his real name is—'

'Rodgers.'

'—Why did he do it? I mean, he had a pretty good job . . .'

'He also had a pretty good collection of debts, it seems,' Goldway told her. 'He'd been gambling heavily, unknown to us, and had lost nearly seven thousand pounds.'

'I did wonder if he had any vices,' Mike put in. 'But gambling was something that didn't occur to me.'

'The bug had bitten him badly. Unless he'd been extraordinarily lucky he could never have hoped to make up his losses in the normal way – say on horse racing or at cards. The Cordoba pendant must have struck him as the answer to his dilemma. No one would dream of suspecting him, and he had all the information and shady contacts at his disposal, an unfortunate but necessary part of his job. In a moment of weakness he must have decided that was the only way out.'

'Yes, the Cordoba pendant!' exclaimed Linda, with mounting enthusiasm. 'Rodgers was connected with the investigations on that robbery case too, wasn't he? I read all about him in that book Mike ordered from the bookshop – the one Nadia Tarrant was reading in the Reference Library.'

'That's right,' confirmed Mike. '. . . Come to think of it, Linda – how did *you* know I suspected Rodgers? I never actually mentioned him by name, and there are quite a few CID men referred to in that book.'

'Oh, darling!' Linda said, beaming. '*You'll* never make a detective! You let your pencil stray on to the page at that particular passage, so I guessed you'd been giving it special attention.'

'Well I'll be damned!'

'But what I don't understand,' she went on as both men burst into laughter, 'is where that poor little wretch Luigi Saltoni fits into the pattern.'

'Saltoni obviously suspected Rodgers, perhaps knew something about him. That's why he made a point of seeing Mike privately, when no police were present,' Goldway explained.

'You mean when I picked him up in my taxi?'

'Yes. We assumed he was just scared of the Law in general,

but in actual fact it could well have been Rodgers in particular who frightened him.'

'And it was, of course, Rodgers who hired some thugs to beat the lad up near his Euston digs,' Mike went on. 'Saltoni's fears were thus justified; and if he recovered consciousness in that ambulance on the way to St Matthew's Hospital he must have nearly had heart failure when he saw who was sitting beside him.'

'So Rodgers was able to get at him in the hospital and make him change his mind. *Of course!* No one else was allowed in to see him. No wonder Saltoni pretended he'd not been telling the truth about Nadia Tarrant.'

'One thing I'd like to know,' Mike said. 'Rodgers murdered Nadia Tarrant at Farnham, but how did he officially cover his tracks and account for having been so conveniently on the spot soon afterwards, to identify the body?'

'All too easily. He simply claimed that he was investigating Hector Staines's background, both at Staines's firm in Guildford and at that pub near Westerdale. That's how he happened to be in the neighbourhood and, of course, we never dreamed of querying that.'

'It all sounds too simple, doesn't it? But, of course, the whole of the Weldon case played right into his hands – he was in charge of the investigations from the beginning so he had every opportunity to tilt the scales in his favour.'

'You mean things like the bloodstained handkerchief that Weldon couldn't account for?' put in Linda. 'Yes, Rodgers must have been responsible for that.'

'And the fact that Nadia Tarrant was supposed to have left the restaurant in Greek Street at about the time Lucy Staines was murdered,' Mike added. 'Of course, she must have left much earlier than that, if she was really with Saltoni at the time – but Rodgers was in a position to avoid probing too deeply into anything that might point to the truth; and he could easily suppress any statements that weren't to his own advantage.'

'One thing I was right about, it seems,' Linda murmured. 'Staines's relationship to Peggy Bedford.'

Goldway nodded. 'Yes, he's admitted that he was trying to persuade the girl to marry him. And he was telling the truth when he denied knowing that he'd been in the Lord Fairfax pub with her. *She* took him there, and he just didn't bother to look at the name of the pub.'

'But that still doesn't explain the mystery of the entry in Lucy Staines's diary,' Linda persisted.

The Superintendent frowned. 'This bit's pure conjecture, since both girls are dead and we can't ask them, but I'm inclined to think that Peggy was a bit embarrassed by having her best girl friend's father nervously hovering on the brink of a proposal. Remember the gap in years. It's my bet that Peggy made a date with Lucy to talk the matter over with her. The place she chose for a nice quiet chat was the Lord Fairfax.'

'On the other hand,' said Mike, 'it could have been an appointment with anyone who knew she had part of the film and who hoped to do a deal with her.'

Linda nodded slowly. 'And whoever it was denied all knowledge of the rendezvous in the diary because he or she wanted to keep out of the limelight. That's understandable. Peggy, for one, must have guessed why Lucy was murdered and was scared that if the police camped on her doorstep they'd find out about her friendship with Larry Boardman.'

'Exactly.'

There was a tap at the door and Mrs Potter came in with more coffee.

Goldway smiled at her and said, 'Mrs Potter, this is excellent coffee, but I must ask you to turn the percolator off or I'll be here all night!'

They all laughed, and when Mrs Potter had gone Linda said in apologetic tones, 'I'll let you go in a moment, John, but I've still got one or two questions up my sleeve! The night Irene Long got plastered and warned Mike not to go down to Reading, she overheard two people talking and fixing up to take Mike for a ride. That must have been Rodgers and Corina, I suppose?'

'Yes. She told us she didn't recognise the voices, but she was fairly drunk at the time anyway,' Mike reminded her. 'It was round about then that my suspicions began to gather weight. Sanders telephoned me the next day. I dare say he was getting pretty worried about the way things were going. After all, he was mixed up in it himself, and so was his girl friend, and Harold Weldon's life was at stake – so it's not surprising if he was over-anxious for news. But it so happened that Rodgers was with me when I took the call. He knew it was Sanders on the phone, and when I made a point of telling Rodgers I'd been warned not to go to Reading he put two and two together and jumped to the conclusion that it was Sanders who'd warned me.'

'Ah, the light is slowly beginning to dawn in my befuddled brain,' Linda said. 'When Sanders was involved in that car accident you guessed it must have been Rodgers who was trying to get rid of him?'

'Exactly!' Mike answered. 'Only the plan nearly boomeranged on me – I didn't know you were going to get hurt too, Linda.'

'Oh, it was all in a good cause, darling!' she said rather smugly. 'Now, if only I could place Corina in all this I think I'd let you two gentlemen get some sleep.'

Mike volunteered the answers. 'Corina was an outsider at first, with a moderately but not entirely clean record. Some of his past was probably known to Rodgers. With this as a capital investment Rodgers must have decided to bank a little more on Corina and slipped the word about Jo's real mission to him. Corina was furious that the Yard were watching his club, but it wasn't he who kidnapped her and beat her up; it was Rodgers.'

'Why did he do it?'

'To throw suspicion on Corina and make us concentrate on La Pergola. You'll remember he even took the pains to have someone with a slight foreign accent do some of the questioning when they put Jo through her third degree. It was very cleverly thought out.'

'What finally made Corina change his mind and come in with us? I mean, he did co-operate in the end, didn't he?' Linda said.

Goldway smiled grimly. 'Like a well-trained circus horse! We simply told him the whole story and put the fear of God in him, including a threat to close down La Pergola if he refused to play.'

Goldway finished his coffee and made signs of leaving. Linda looked so disappointed that he sank back on to the settee with a resigned grin.

'Just one more question, John! Why did Hector Staines install that listening apparatus above Irene Long's flat? Did he think she might be working for Bannister?'

'I don't think so. But his partner-in-crime was Sanders, and I don't think there was much love lost between the two.

Staines didn't trust his partner, and in order to make sure he wasn't being double-crossed he decided to listen in on the scene where Victor Sanders spent most of his evenings – at Irene Long's flat.'

'That makes sense,' decided Linda.

Goldway eased himself off the settee and asked, 'What are you going to do now, Mike? If I remember rightly you were off on a holiday to the South of France when this business started?'

Mike glanced guiltily at Linda. 'Er . . . yes, that was the plan, but I'm afraid the holiday's off, at least for the time being.'

Linda looked at her husband. 'This is news to me, Mike. What's happened?'

Mike said, 'I meant to tell you, Linda. The Editor of the *Tribune* has asked me to write a series of articles on the Weldon case . . .'

Linda shook her head. 'The Weldon case is finished – tomorrow afternoon we leave for Cannes!'

'Now look here,' said Mike, glancing at the Superintendent, 'who's the boss around here?'

Linda smiled. It was a very sweet smile. 'What a silly question, Mike! Why you are, dear. You know that. You always have been.'

'Then I write the articles,' said Mike, pushing out his chest. 'And don't argue, darling.'

Mike did write the articles. On the beach at Cannes.

Paul Temple and the Nightingale

Paul Temple first heard of 'The Nightingale' when he was
sitting in his Club drinking a dry martini. A friendly hand
patted him on the shoulder and a familiar voice said: 'So
this is where you spend your evenings, Mr Temple!'

Temple smiled and shook the outstretched hand. 'This is
the first time I've been in the Club for ages. Sir Graham,'
he said. 'And I wouldn't be here now if Steve wasn't having
a massage.'

Sir Graham Forbes laughed. 'What's your wife's massage
in aid of, Temple?'

Temple said: 'We travelled back from the south of France
last night and Steve's got a touch of fibrositis. You know
those Continental sleepers. Sir Graham?'

Forbes sank into the nearby armchair. 'Things have been
happening while you've been basking in the sun,' he said
quietly. 'Why, I don't suppose you've even heard of "The
Nightingale".'

'The Nightingale?'

The head of Scotland Yard nodded. 'The man's a menace,
Temple. He's robbed ten flats in twelve days and got away
with nearly £90,000 worth of jewellery.'

'What sort of a man is he, Sir Graham?'

'We don't know, Temple,' said Forbes seriously. 'No one's even caught a glimpse of the fellow.'

'When did you first hear of him?'

'He broke into Lord Arleston's flat about a month ago,' said Forbes. 'Arleston was giving a dinner party and didn't hear a sound. That dinner party cost his lordship the best part of £17,000.'

'Does he confine his activities to the West End, Sir Graham?'

'Nearly always,' said Forbes. 'And curiously enough it's generally the Berkeley Square area.' He smiled. 'That's why we nicknamed him "The Nightingale".'

'Haven't you anything to go on – not a clue of any sort?'

There was a curious expression on Sir Graham's face; he looked puzzled.

'I just don't understand it, Temple,' he said quietly. 'The fellow's unbelievably careless and yet he slips through our fingers every time.'

'What do you mean by careless, Sir Graham? Does he leave his fingerprints all over the place?'

Forbes laughed. 'It's not quite as bad as that,' he said. 'But he left one of his gloves behind at Lord Arleston's, and when he broke into Donald Marshbank's place he was actually smoking a pipe. He tapped it out on the window-sill.'

Paul Temple smiled. 'You certainly seem to have your hands full, Sir Graham,' he said. '"The Nightingale" sounds a very odd bird!'

It was a quarter to eight when Temple arrived at Berkeley Grange and walked up the four flights of stairs to his flat on the fourth floor.

The key was in the lock and Temple's hand on the handle when the door was suddenly thrown open and the novelist found himself facing a tall, rather serious-looking girl in the late twenties. The girl wore glasses, was carrying a large handbag, and looked annoyed.

'I'm Miss Allen, Mrs Temple's masseuse,' said the girl. 'I'm waiting for Mrs Temple.'

Temple frowned. 'I thought my wife's appointment was for seven o'clock?'

The girl nodded and tucked her handbag firmly under her left arm.

'So did I,' she said, unable to conceal the note of asperity in her voice. 'But when I got out of the lift I bumped into Mrs Temple and she told me she had another appointment and would be back in a quarter of an hour.' The girl looked at her watch. 'That was precisely forty minutes ago!'

Temple led her back into the lounge.

'Miss Allen,' he said, 'someone ought to have warned you. My wife's never punctual.'

Miss Allen said: 'Yes, well I have other patients, Mr Temple, and I can't afford to keep them waiting. Perhaps you'll tell your wife to give me a ring if she wishes to make another appointment.' She turned towards the door.

Temple took a firm grip on her arm and guided her across to the cocktail cabinet.

'I know exactly how you feel, young lady, but don't let it get you down!' He picked up the whisky decanter. 'What you need is a good stiff drink.'

The girl hesitated for a moment and then suddenly laughed and put her handbag down on the corner of the cocktail cabinet. 'Whisky isn't much in my line,' she said. 'But if you've a gin and tonic handy . . .'

'By Timothy,' thought Temple, 'she's a jolly good looking girl when she smiles.'

He replaced the whisky decanter, walked across the lounge, and out into the kitchen. When he returned a few moments later, carrying tonic waters and a bottle of gin, he noticed that the girl had picked up her handbag and was standing with her back to the cocktail cabinet, her eyes on the bedroom door.

He stood watching her for a little while then he put down the bottles and opened the palm of his left hand. He was holding a button.

'Did you drop this button, Miss Allen?'

The girl turned and looked down at the button: it was about the size of a half-penny and looked as if it had been torn from a man's sports jacket. She shook her head. 'It's off a man's jacket,' she said.

'It was placed near the service door,' Temple said, 'to give the impression that it was a man who entered the flat and not a woman.'

'I'm afraid I don't follow you.' She opened her handbag and turned towards the mirror above the cocktail cabinet. It looked as if she was about to produce a powder compact and powder her nose.

Temple said: 'It's really quite simple. "The Nightingale" isn't a man at all.' He smiled. 'You deliberately placed the glove at Lord Arleston's and planted the pipe tobacco at Donald Marshbank's.'

The girl knew that the game was up and she turned and moved away from the cocktail cabinet. Instead of a powder compact she was holding a small automatic pistol.

'There's no need for any unpleasantness,' she said, pointing the revolver at Temple's chest. 'I suggest you join your wife in the bedroom.'

208

'What's happened to my wife?'

The girl crossed in front of the cocktail cabinet and, with the revolver still pointing at Temple, opened the bedroom door.

Temple could see his wife lying on the bed; her hands and feet bound, a silk handkerchief tied round her mouth.

The girl said: 'Before you join your wife, Mr Temple, perhaps you'll explain why you suspected me?'

Temple shrugged his shoulders and took out his cigarette case.

'Your reference to the lift gave you away,' he said casually. 'I knew you couldn't possibly have come up by the lift because the confounded thing's out of order; it's been out of order for three weeks.'

'You're quite right,' said the girl. 'I came in by the service door just as the masseuse was leaving. I heard your wife saying goodbye to her in the hall and . . .' She never completed the sentence because at that precise moment Temple threw the cigarette case.

As the case hit the girl's shoulder Temple jumped forward and caught the butt of the revolver with the side of his hand. He heard the explosion and saw the girl stagger back towards the bedroom door. He leaped forward. It was to be the knock-out blow to end all knock-out blows.

Suddenly, at the very last moment, he remembered that he was a gentleman.

Late that night, when they were sitting in front of the fire, Steve said: 'I began to wonder if you were ever going to turn up, Paul.'

'I didn't leave my publishers' until a quarter past six,' said Temple. 'And then I dropped into the Club for an hour.' He smiled. 'It's a good job I did, otherwise I shouldn't have seen Sir Graham and heard all about "The Nightingale".'

His wife said: 'Inspector Vosper looked delighted when he arrested her. I think now he's really convinced you're a genius, Paul.'

'Don't you think I'm a genius, darling?'

'It was certainly clever of you to notice that slip – but I really think there's something you ought to know.'

Temple looked puzzled.

Steve was smiling at him; there was a mischievous twinkle in her eyes. 'While you were at your publishers' this afternoon something happened.'

'What do you mean?'

Steve laughed. 'Take a deep breath, darling,' she said. 'They repaired the lift!'

BY THE SAME AUTHOR

Beware of Johnny Washington

When a gang of desperate criminals begins leaving calling cards inscribed '*With the Compliments of Johnny Washington*', the real Johnny Washington is encouraged by an attractive newspaper columnist to throw in his lot with the police. Johnny, an American 'gentleman of leisure' who has settled at a quiet country house in Kent to enjoy the fishing, soon finds himself involved with the mysterious Horatio Quince, a retired schoolmaster who is on the trail of the gang's unscrupulous leader, the elusive 'Grey Moose'.

Best known for creating *Paul Temple* for BBC radio in 1938, Francis Durbridge's prolific output of crime and mystery stories, encompassing plays, radio, television, films and books, made him a household name for more than 50 years. A new radio character, *Johnny Washington Esquire*, hit the airwaves in 1949, leading to the publication of this one-off novel in 1951.

This Detective Club classic is introduced by writer and bibliographer Melvyn Barnes, author of *Francis Durbridge: A Centenary Appreciation*, who reveals how Johnny Washington's only literary outing was actually a reworking of Durbridge's own *Send for Paul Temple*.

Send for Paul Temple

In the dead of night, a watchman is brutally attacked and with his dying breath cries out, 'The Green Finger!' It is the latest in a series of robberies to leave Scotland Yard mystified and the press clamouring that they 'Send for Paul Temple!' Aided by a young female reporter known as Steve Trent, Paul is faced with solving a deepening and widening mystery . . .

Send for Paul Temple was the first of ten straight novelisations of Francis Durbridge's phenomenally popular Paul Temple radio serials. As well as conquering the airwaves between 1938 and 1968, Paul Temple featured in films, television series, one-off novels, short stories and newspaper strips, and these original books remain as compulsive as ever.

'Paul Temple commands a greater audience than any film actor or stage star. Temple's adventures are listened to by millions of people all over the world. Temple is the modern Sherlock Holmes.'

—*Evening Standard*

BY THE SAME AUTHOR

Paul Temple and the Tyler Mystery

Outside Oxford, police officers find a woman's body in the boot of a stolen car. Approached by Scotland Yard to investigate, Paul Temple is reluctant to get involved, until he discovers that he knows the prime suspect and is faced with yet more murders.

The Tyler Mystery was the first Paul Temple original novel, written by Francis Durbridge and Douglas Rutherford under the pseudonym 'Paul Temple'. Set in Temple's sophisticated world of chilled cocktails and fast cars, where men wore cravats and women were chic, it was presented as 'a story which could only be told in book form and has never been presented on the radio' and propelled the smooth sleuth and his glamorous wife Steve into – of course – mortal danger!

'Paul Temple gives thrills, suspense, and excitement for all.'
—*Daily Mail*

Design for Murder

The Assistant Commissioner of Scotland Yard visits a retired detective with the news that an old adversary has struck again, strangling an innocent girl. Wyatt is reluctant to return to police work, but then another body is found – this time at his own home, with a chilling message: 'With the compliments of Mr Rossiter'.

In *Design for Murder*, Francis Durbridge adapted his longest Paul Temple serial, *Paul Temple and the Gregory Affair*, into a full-length novel. All the obligatory elements from the thrilling radio episodes were present, but in a new twist, he renamed the principal characters: Paul and Steve Temple became Lionel and Sally Wyatt, and 'Mr Rossiter' replaced the villainous Gregory. Reprinted for the first time in 66 years, fans of Francis Durbridge and of Paul Temple can finally relive this ingenious adventure.

Includes the exclusive 1946 *Radio Times* short story 'Paul Temple's White Christmas'.

Back Room Girl

Retiring to No Man's Cove in Cornwall to write his memoirs, crime reporter Roy Benton discovers that a disused tin mine has become a research station for a secret weapons project. Karen Silvers, in charge of operations, reluctantly accepts that Benton's experience could help her fight a sinister organisation intent on stealing their plans.

Having adapted five of his *Paul Temple* radio serials into successful novelisations, in 1950 Francis Durbridge decided to try his hand at writing his first original novel. *Back Room Girl* bore all the hallmarks of the famous Paul Temple stories, an outlandish mixture of mystery, glamour and suspense, in a book that was never reprinted and so became an enigma to his many fans – until now.

Includes an introduction by bibliographer Melvyn Barnes plus two rare short stories written for Christmas annuals: 'Light-Fingers' and 'A Present from Paul Temple'.

BY THE SAME AUTHOR

Dead to the World

Photographer and amateur detective Philip Holt is asked to investigate the unexplained murder of an American student at an English university. With a postcard signed 'Christopher' and the boy's father's missing signet ring as his only leads, Holt's investigation soon snowballs into forgery, blackmail, smuggling . . . and more murder.

Dead to the World is Francis Durbridge's novelisation of his radio serial *Paul Temple and the Jonathan Mystery*, rewriting the Paul and Steve Temple characters as Philip Holt and his secretary Ruth Sanders. This new edition is introduced by bibliographer Melvyn Barnes and includes the Paul Temple Christmas story 'The Ventriloquist's Doll'.